My Secret To Keep

DANIELLE SILER

Rising Storm
ISBN-13: 978-0615852546
ISBN-10: 0615852548

DEDICATION

To my beautiful daughters Jasmine and Jaylen, mommy loves you more than anything else in this world. You are my inspiration and motivation to keep breaking these glass ceilings. To my husband Chad, I never thought I would find my other half until I found you. To my mother Suzette Siler, my grandparents Yvonne and Jazz Siler, and the rest of my Siler and Graves families thank you for always encouraging and supporting my dreams. Last, but not least, thank you to my fans for your continued love and support!

CONTENTS

MY SECRET TO KEEP

ACKNOWLEDGMENTS

I want to acknowledge God for giving me this gift and the means to share it with the world! I am humbled every day by your grace and mercy

Sometimes when people retell history, facts get lost. Whether accidental or intentional, some people skew the facts. It is a belief held by some that those sold into slavery were dumb, worthless and of no great importance. Some people believe the lives of those captured slaves were an inconsequential state of existence. These are both false beliefs.

Many that found themselves thrust into the barbarism of slavery, with all its related atrocities, were, in fact, the elite, the educated, the kings, the philosophers, and warriors. Their enemies perceived these people as a threat to whatever agenda their enemy had.

Because of this, their enemies sold them into slavery as a punishment; a means to get rid of an opposing adversary or solely for the profit of greed. Yes, some were unfortunate enough to be caught and forced into slavery, but others were placed there by one of their own.

However, they came to be a slave, no crime ever committed could justify the treatment and inhumane conditions they were made to endure. The unfathomable belief that one person should have the right to own, maim or murder another human being under the guise that other human being is your property is unconscionable.

Further, to twist the words found in the bible or any other religious text to justify your offensive behavior is not only contrary to the work of God, but is a direct homage to the Devil himself. The horror of slavery and loss suffered by its institution will undoubtedly leave an indelible scar on the lives of those forced to endure it. It is of no consequence that God's law stated it was inhumane or that eventually, man's rule said it was unjust; those facts were not enough to cure the cancer of hatred that still coursed through the hearts of man. No salve of justice can heal the wounds that slavery left on humanity's very soul.

My Secret to Keep is the second installment in the Secret Chronicles. In the first book, Secrets on Tobacco Road, we were introduced to the Devereux, Marchand, and Jean-Baptiste (Monet) families. The former two were affluent families in New Orleans, and the last was the slave family that worked for the Devereuxs.

The patriarchs of the Devereux and Marchand families, Peter Devereux and Alexander Marchand, forced their heirs, John Devereux and Helena Marchand, to marry in a plan to merge their power structure. Unfortunately, John Devereux was in love with Marie Jean Baptiste, his childhood friend who was also a slave on his plantation. Helena also grew up as both John and Marie's childhood friend, but as she grew she developed an unhealthy obsession with John and a deep resentment and hatred for Marie.

Helena's hatred grew darker when she realized that her soon to be husband and Marie shared a forbidden night of passion on the eve of their wedding announcement, which resulted in twin boys. In a jealous rage, she, in turn, had an affair that led to an infection that rendered her barren. Although not responsible for how Helena contracted the disease, Marie's mother Sarah mixed potions that assisted the condition of being infertile. Sarah was a direct descendant of the infamous voodoo priestess Marie Laveau. Sarah used her family legacy to punish Helena and anyone else who crossed her.

To explain Marie's pregnancy, Peter Devereux forced her to marry a fellow slave named Thomas Childress. When the twins were born, one with the darker skin of Marie and the other with fair skin like John; Peter Devereux took the lighter child to be raised by John and Helena and left the darker one to be reared as a slave by Marie and Thomas.

After inheriting a Tobacco plantation in NC from an estranged uncle's passing, Peter moved his entire family to hide their secrets. When civil unrest in the country led to a war that caused these families' secrets to be dangerous and Marie to become a widow; Peter sent Marie, John and the twins to Canada. Helena had fled back to New Orleans before the war started. Although Marie and John fled together with their children, they did not reveal to the boys that they were twins, nor that Marie and John were their parents.

My Secret to keep picks up with these character's lives after everything they endured in Secrets on Tobacco Road, but it also introduces some additional characters, and backstories to characters fans came to love and hate in the first novel.

Chapter One

Heavy is the Head that wears the Crown

Winter 1813

In the early 1800s, there was a mighty Houngan Asogwe (High Priest), and Mambo (Priestess) named Obataye and Grace St. Croix. Best known as Papa Obie and Mama Grace, this Priest and Priestess' powers were legendary in their native country of Haiti. Their skills bred both fear and jealousy, so they were not short on enemies.

One day Grace was awakened from an afternoon nap, by the pleas of a frantic young woman.

"Mambo, I need your counsel," the young woman said as she stood at the entrance of Grace and Obataye's hut.

Grace, who was six months pregnant at the time invited her to come in. "What is it that worries you, my child?" Grace inquired.

"Oh Mama Grace, I am troubled. My husband died, and I had no one to take care of my five children and me." The girl said.

"So, you have come to seek my assistance in finding someone to marry you?" Grace asked.

"No Mambo, I have found a great and powerful man who said that he would marry me and take care of my children and me. He said that I must first kill his enemy to prove my loyalty to him." The girl replied.

Confused as to what the girl wanted, Grace quizzed. "So, what is it that you want me to do?"

"Die Mambo!" the girl shouted as she drove a knife into Grace's chest.

Grace was able to force the girl off of her so that the puncture was not as severe as intended, but Grace was still wounded and bleeding. As Grace lay on the floor with her blood pooling from her body, the girl ran to get Obataye (the real target).

"Papa Obie, come quick. Mama Grace is hurt!" The girl shouted as she ran towards Obataye, who was gathering herbs for a potion.

Obataye ran as fast as he could back to their hut and he found Grace bleeding on the floor. He was so focused on getting to her that he didn't even see his soon to be assailants hiding in the corner.

As soon as Obataye entered the tent, two men grabbed him. Each man held one of Obataye's massive arms, and he still tossed them about the room like rag dolls. When it seemed, he was about to free himself entirely, the girl blew a fine black powder into Obataye's face, and he fell to the ground unconscious.

When he awoke, he and Grace were on a slave ship bound for America. The deplorable conditions of the slave ship made for unsafe travels for even the healthiest of slaves, but Grace's delicate health and injuries from her attack made it deadly for her.

Obataye knew that his wife and their unborn child's life were in danger, and he did the only thing he could do. He called on a powerful loa (spirit) named Papa Legba and asked him for his protection.

"Papa Legba hear my cry. Restore my wife's health and protect our unborn child. Restore my powers and make them greater than before, so that I may avenge this smite to my family." Obataye prayed.

There in the middle of the slave ship appeared an old man, with dark skin, shoulder-length dreadlocks, wearing a top hat and smoking a pipe. His eyes were red as hot coals, and he carried a staff.

"Who calls for me?" Legba asked

"I called for you great loa. I humbly ask that you grant my request, protect my family and not only restore but magnify my powers." Obataye answered.

Papa Legba walked over to Grace and then looked back at Obataye. "You ask for a great task Houngan, your wife is near death and so are your daughters," Legba stated.

"Daughters?" Obataye asked with confusion.

"Yes Houngan, your wife is carrying double blessings, both minutes away from their final breaths," Legba replied.

"Save them great loa. Save my family, and I will repay your gifts with my life." Obataye offered.

The old man began to laugh and said "Houngan. I have no use for your life and for a feat this great the cost is greater than merely the time you have left on this earth."

Desperation gripped Obataye as he watched the very life slip out of Grace's body. "Name your price, great loa, and you shall surely have it." Obataye pleaded.

Blowing smoke rings from his lips, Legba responded, "I will grant your requests Houngan, but the price is your soul."

Obataye agreed to Legba's terms with no hesitation. In his eyes, his soul was a small price to pay to save his family. Legba placed his palms on top of Grace's wound, and it began to heal, he then put his hands on her belly.

Legba felt the powerful energy, and he looked at Obataye with a big smile. "Ah now these little ones are going to be great Mambos one day. Even as they struggle to breathe, their will to live is strong. I shall be watching over their growth very closely." Legba said. As requested, he granted Obataye's wish in exchange for his soul.

Chapter Two

Slavery, The American Nightmare

Spring 1814

The St. Croixs arrived in America and were immediately sent to auction in New Orleans. Obataye and Grace stood naked on an auction block alongside other slaves that survived the voyage. Once respected and feared, now people poked and prodded them like animals.

"Step right up folks; we have some good strong stock that just came in from Haiti." An auctioneer shouted as he pointed to the slaves.

"How much for this one? He is a big buck. I bet I could get a lot of work out of him." A man asked looking at Obataye.

"Bidding for him starts at $600" the auctioneer replied.

"I bet he would be able to breed me some strong stock once I find a wench to mate him with." The man said aloud, still inspecting Obataye and marveling at his muscular physique.

"Why yes sir; in fact, the wench beside him is carrying his child right now! So, if you buy'em both, it will be like getting three slaves for the price of two! The auctioneer exclaimed.

"Is that right? Ok, I will give you $1000 for both." The man offered with money in hand.

"Sold! Now step this way to claim your stock and get your bill of sale." Replied the auctioneer. He pocketed his ill-gotten gains and moved on to the next slave.

And just like that, Obataye and Grace were sold into slavery. Upon their arrival to their new home, Obataye made Grace a promise.

"My sweet Gracie, I promise on my life, that I will never let harm come to you or our daughters." Obataye pledged.

Through tear-stained eyes Grace assured, "Nor will I, my love.

It didn't take the other slaves on the plantation long to realize Grace and Obataye were no ordinary slaves. Their gifts and station in their former life was a secret only to their new masters.

Two months after their arrival, Grace had twin baby girls named Tabitha and Sadie on April 10, 1814. A midwife who was also from Haiti and familiar with the St. Croixs, delivered them.

The midwife felt the power of the twins immediately as she ushered them into this world; but as the twins grew, so did their abilities. When they were very young, their natural gifts had attracted the attention of Papa Legba.

Legba was intrigued by them and offered to give them powers beyond belief in exchange for their soul. Tabitha would have eagerly accepted, but Sadie refused to sell her soul to the darkness. Legba told them he would come back to see them on their 20th birthday, and they could give their final decision then.

As the twins became teenagers, the slave master took an interest in Tabitha and sought to make her his concubine. He came for her one night and got more than he expected. Although Tabitha was a house slave, she had crept down to the slave quarters to stay with her family that night. She had a sinking feeling in the pit of her stomach all that day, each time she crossed paths with the master. The look he gave her solidified her feelings, and she was not about to be there when he came.

The slave master went to Tabitha's room later that night but found she was not there. So, he searched the house and still came up empty-handed. Then it dawned on him that she may be seeking protection with her family.

"Humph, silly wench thinks that she can hide behind her mommy and daddy. I own her and them too! Tonight, I am going to taste her sweet nectar, and no man will stop me!" The master laughed.

Drunk and feeling he had waited long enough to experience Tabitha, the slave master crept into the slave quarters were she, and Sadie lay sleeping.

"Tonight wench, you are going to be mine finally." He laughed to himself. But before he could lay one hand on her, Obataye picked up the master and threw him to the ground. He hit his head on the edge of a rock which killed him instantly.

Although Obataye took the master's body and laid it in the woods, the slave master's wife still blamed Tabitha for his disappearance. She knew her husband was going to Tabitha that night and she knew that Obataye was very protective of his family.

After learning of the discovery of her husband's body the following evening, the slave master's wife instructed her teenaged sons to drag Obataye to the tree in the middle of the plantation and hang him. She wanted his body to be discovered the next morning when everyone awoke, but when they came to get him, Obataye overpowered both young men and strangled them between his massive arms. Grace then tied another noose on the opposite end of the rope and threw the line over the tree meant to hang Obataye.

When the slave master's wife awoke the next morning to reveal in Obataye's family's pain, she found her sons hanging in his place. The slave master's wife screamed in anguish as she looked at her sons' lifeless bodies swinging in the breeze. She was furious and demanded to know where Obataye was, but there was no answer. Obataye had fled into the woods that same night and promised his family he would return to them when he found a safe place for them.

The slave master's wife turned her anger to Tabitha. She saw Tabitha as the source of her pain, and she was going to make her suffer for that.

"You, Black she-devil! My husband was so obsessed with you that it cost him his life and now the lives of my sons! You will not spend another day on this plantation, and you will never see your family again!" She shouted.

The master's wife had intended to hang Tabitha's father to make her suffer, and when she did not get that satisfaction, she would make the rest of Tabitha's family suffer. The very next day, the slave master's wife sold Tabitha, but Sadie and Grace remained at the plantation.

With the slave master and his sons dead and no one to help his widow, she could not maintain the plantation. She fell on hard times and to ease her financial burden; she sold more of her slaves. In 1833, she sold Sadie and Grace to Dr. Leonard Louis Nicholas LaLaurie and his wife, Delphine.

The Devil has Two Faces

Spring 1834

Once Sadie and Grace settled into the LaLaurie's home, it didn't take long for Grace to find that Delphine had a curiosity with voodoo. Grace used that information to endear herself to Delphine. She mixed various fake potions that she told Delphine would keep her beautiful and wealthy. Those counterfeit medicines protected both Grace and Sadie. It did not, however, protect them from witnessing the horrors Delphine did to other slaves.

Delphine had a sadistic appetite for torture, which she satiated by inflicting unspeakable pain on her slaves. Her cruelty was not spared on her daughters either, especially her daughter Borquita. Delphine sadistically beat her daughters for giving the slaves food, water or any compassion.

Delphine turned the top level of her Royal Street mansion into a full-fledged torture chamber. There were slaves whose limbs had been twisted and broken to resemble crabs or other creatures. She pulled one of her slave's intestines from their body and tied them around their waist like a belt. There were also slaves who had human and animal feces shoved into their mouths and then sewn shut.

No act was too horrid for Delphine LaLaurie, and she kept her victims confined there in her little museum of madness. Grace knew that Delphine's reign of terror had to end and one day fate had given her just the way to do it.

Grace noticed that she was being followed on a trip into town to shop for groceries. When she turned onto a secluded alleyway, her heart stopped. Standing in front of her was the child she thought she would never see again, Tabitha.

"Tabitha? Is that you my child?" Grace asked.

With tears of joy running down her face, Tabitha replied "Yes mama."

Grace ran over to Tabitha and wrapped her in an embrace she never thought would occur outside of her dreams.

"Where have you been? I tried to find out where you were, but I lost track of you. I also asked if anyone knew anything about your father, but I found nothing of him either." Grace stated.

"Oh, mama I have so much to tell you," Tabitha responded.

Tabitha told Grace how Obataye had come back to the plantation looking for them and the slaves told him the masters sold everyone to different people. He had built a cabin deep in the Bayou, and he was planning to bring his family home. She also told her about what happened to her once the masters sold her to another plantation, and her journey to find her father.

Tabitha had grown to be very powerful, even more powerful than her mother. Her owners sold Tabitha many times, but each time she was sold the families all met with tragic ends. The slave masters were all beguiled by her beauty. Her flawless mahogany skin and long thick black hair which she kept braided atop her head, gave her the appearance of royalty. Her confidence and power over her masters bred jealousy and hatred in their wives. One by one each slave master fell to her charms, and each wife tried to make her pay the price, only to meet with some ill fate.

Finally, one slave master's wife had planned to kill Tabitha. She had heard the rumors about Tabitha and the misfortune that followed for any family who acquired her, but rage so blinded her that she ignored her better judgment.

Tabitha knew that her mistress was going to try to kill her, so she put white snake root in the family's nightly glass of milk and made sure that all the overseers had a drink before bed as well. People would assume the family's death came from the cow eating the poisonous plant causing its milk to become tainted (which was commonly known as milk poisoning). To further this theory, when Tabitha went out to feed the cattle earlier that day, she added some white snake root to their feed.

That night as the poisonous cocktail worked its way through the family's system, Tabitha made her escape and encouraged the rest of the slaves to run as well. With all the slaves gone and everyone else on the plantation dead, no one noticed anything for days.

Before leaving, she stole the master's seal and some paper. She had already written her freedom papers and those of as many other slaves that she could (including her father, sister, and mother). She gave the seal and remaining sheets to one of the other slaves she knew could read and write to assist with drafting papers for the others when they made it to freedom.

Tabitha went on her way in search of her father. When she found him, he took her to their new home deep in the bayou.

Many people, slaves, and Whites included came to her and Obataye seeking their assistance and their counsel. In turn, they would inquire about Sadie and Grace's whereabouts. One patron revealed that the LaLauries bought Sadie and Grace and Tabitha began to search for them. Once she tracked down the mansion, she waited to find a way to contact Grace or Sadie. When she saw Grace leave the house headed for the market, she knew that was her chance.

Grace informed Tabitha of the atrocities that were committed by Delphine, and they devised a plan. Late that night, on April 10, 1834, the cook (whom Delphine kept chained to the stove) started a fire. When bystanders attempted to evacuate the slave quarters, they were refused keys to enter. The bystanders then broke down the door and found slaves mutilated so severely they hardly looked human.

When the news spread, an angry mob obliterated the mansion brick by brick until hardly anything remained. Before the crowd could lay waste to the LaLauries, the LaLauries' daughter Borquita (who unbeknownst to the LaLauries was in on the coup) led them to a "safe house" deep in the bayou, with their trusted slaves Grace and Sadie along with them.

Before they were separated, the twins were being trained to be powerful voodoo priestesses. Sadie was drawn more to the art of healing, but Tabitha liked the art of revenge. They were twin sisters, but they were as different as night and day.

Sadie embraced the light and Tabitha adopted the dark. Both girls were born with an extraordinary gift. Knowing the horrors that Madam LaLaurie put her slaves through broke the twins' hearts, and they longed to end their suffering. Sadie wanted to heal it, Tabitha tried to avenge it; all agreed it had to stop.

People assumed that the LaLauries fled to Paris with their daughters when the mob destroyed their home, but they were only half right. Delphine's daughters despised their mother and stepfather almost as much as the slaves did. So, they lured their parents to the cabin in the woods where Tabitha and Obataye delivered their own brand of justice. Delphine's daughters then took the fortune of their despicable parents and fled to Paris, making others believe that their parents were with them. Filled with rage over hearing of the slave's treatment, Tabitha and Obataye gave the LaLauries a taste of their own medicine.

"Ah, Madam LaLaurie welcome to our humble abode," Obataye said in his thick Haitian accent. "We have some extra special treats in store for our extra special guests!" he laughed.

"Who are you?" Delphine quizzed.

With a widening smile, Obataye answered. "Who am I? I am your host; and as such, I have exhausted much effort to make sure you feel right at home. See my wife and daughter have filled me in on how you have a taste for the Macabre. You tortured all the slaves unfortunate enough to be in your care, by twisting their bodies and mutilating them for your enjoyment. And your spineless husband stood by and allowed these things to happen. So, I feel it only fitting that you experience the same hospitality while you are in my care."

Since Obataye felt that Delphine's husband Leonard allowed her to commit these deplorable acts because he had no backbone, he made Leonard's spine twist so that he appeared to be doing a backbend. He bent his arms and legs in the shape of an oval and made him walk on his hands and feet like a four-legged animal. Then, he twisted his neck so that his head was facing forward.

When Delphine saw this, she turned white as a ghost and began to cry and beg for mercy.

"Oh my God, please don't hurt me. Please, I am begging you to show mercy on me!" Delphine cried.

"Shh Mon Cherie. No, no, no. There is no need to call on God; he has no use for you. You have no soul to save. And as for mercy, how about I promise to show you the same compassion that you showed all your slaves. Huh? Obataye said with a sinister laugh.

Delphine started to cry again, then Tabitha came to her in a comforting tone offering Delphine what she thought was water.

"Do not fret Madam LaLaurie; my father is not going to hurt you."

Drying her tears and drinking the liquid down, Delphine asked: "He's not?"

"No of course not, he would never hurt a woman. No matter how despicable she is. That is what I am here for." Tabitha said with a devilish grin and evil stare.

Delphine dropped the glass, writhing in pain, as she felt like her body was being twisted and stretched. Tabitha viewed Delphine as a snake, so she made her outward appearance just as hideous as her soul. Tabitha laughed and watched Delphine's body twist. Delphine's arms were fused to her sides, and her legs were melted together with hot burning tar. Her tongue was split in two like a fork and she was made to slither on her belly like a snake.

Although Sadie could think of no one who deserved punishment more than the LaLauries, she didn't delight in their suffering as much as the rest of her family. She also knew that as much as she loved reuniting with them, she would not make a pact with Legba as they did. Sadie knew that she would see him again. After all, they were all together, and it was the twins' 20th birthday; the day their powers reached their full potential, and the day they would have to choose the light or the dark.

Just as Sadie predicted, Legba did show up for the twins' birthday, and he again asked for them to choose. Tabitha followed the path of her parents and adopted the dark, Sadie picked the light.

In 1836 Sadie married an emancipated slave named Louis Martineau and they had one son. Louis worked as a blacksmith and Sadie worked for a wealthy family called the Marchands caring for their newborn daughter they named Helena.

A Mind is a Terrible Thing to Lose

1862

When Helena Marchand Devereux returned to New Orleans, she thought returning to familiar surroundings would help her forget about everything that happened at the Devereux plantation. She was wrong.

Helena's family inquired about why she had returned; and why she returned without her husband and son. She told them that she wasn't ready to talk about it, so they gave her some time.

For the first few months, Helena's family tried to rationalize their daughter's strange behavior. They assumed she was having trouble adjusting to being back home without her son and husband; but as Helena's condition worsened, her family became very concerned about her.

Helena was plagued by nightmares that left her paralyzed with fear and waking up in a cold sweat. Even though Sarah was hundreds of miles away in North Carolina, she hadn't wholly released her grip on Helena. Sarah knew that Helena could be spiteful and vindictive, so she remained connected to her, just in case Helena decided to tell anyone about the Devereux family secrets.

The memories of the hell Helena endured after she unwittingly made Sarah her enemy were seared in Helena's mind forever. Some nights she slept without nightmares, but those nights were few and far between. Most nights Helena drifted between feeling like she was drowning, to feeling like she was being burned alive.

During the day, Helena fluctuated between being paranoid and walking around like a zombie. Her parents were beside themselves with worry. They called on every doctor from every corner of Louisiana to try to find a cure for her puzzling ailment. When the doctors could see no physical reason for her peculiar demeanor, they figured it must be mental.

There was a strange and eerie feeling surrounding the Marchand plantation since Helena had arrived. The staff heard Helena waking in the night with terrible tortured screams.

During the day Helena would sometimes fluctuate between drifting into a trance-like state and being so paranoid that she often looked over her shoulder. She jumped at the least little sound; and she told her parents that she felt like there was a presence that followed her everywhere, even into her dreams.

Alexander and Olivia Marchand were so distraught over what to do about their daughter's unusual behavior; they became desperate and open to anything that may end Helena's suffering.

Early one morning, Olivia heard her daughter having a conversation in her room. She sounded agitated; and when Olivia opened the door, she saw a hysterical Helena rushing about the room as if she were running from something.

"Who are you talking to sweetheart?" Olivia asked as she watched Helena peer out of the window while frantically wringing her hands.

"Did you see her mother?" Helena asked with wide eyes.

"See who Helena? There is nothing there." Olivia said with a look of distress.

"The woman; there was a woman in the room with me. She looked like a slave, but she had eyes that were pure white and soulless, and she walked right through the wall and onto the street!" Helena said visibly shaking.

Gently grabbing her daughter by the shoulders and turning Helena to face her, Olivia said "Helena darling you are starting to scare me. I think it's time we called Dr. Bastian."

Helena pulled away from her mother and retreated to the other side of the room. She cowered in the corner with her back to the wall and screamed "I am not crazy! I saw her mother! She follows me. Everywhere I go she is haunting me!"

Olivia fought back the tears as she watched her child's mental health disintegrate before her eyes. She kneeled, took Helena by the hands and helped her to her feet. Olivia wrapped her arms around her daughter to try to calm her and then guided Helena over to the bed to lie down.

"Rest now Cher, I will fetch the doctor, and he will make you all better," Olivia said as she kissed Helena on the forehead and set out to summon Dr. Bastian.

Dr. Bastian was a young, exceedingly egotistical psychiatrist, with a God complex. He felt he was abreast of all the latest cutting-edge techniques in psychiatric medicine and planned to make quite the name for himself in his field. He was tall and strikingly good looking with chiseled features and enchanting blue eyes.

Dr. Bastian was a proponent of scientific explanations and pharmaceutical solutions, so he erred on the side of over-prescribing medicine. When he arrived at the Marchand plantation, Olivia greeted him at the door.

"Thank you for coming to see us, Dr. Bastian, right this way," Olivia said as she led him to Helena's room.

"It's no bother madam; from what you described you made a wise decision to request my services." Dr. Bastian replied with apparent arrogance.

As Dr. Bastian and Olivia entered Helena's room, they saw her lying in bed staring blankly into space. Dr. Bastian sauntered over to Helena who showed no sign that she was even conscious of anyone entering the room.

"Hello, Helena. I am Dr. David Bastian, and your mother has asked me to come and check on you. She said you haven't been feeling well since your arrival from North Carolina. Can you tell me a little about what is upsetting you?" quizzed Dr. Bastian.

Snapping into a temporary moment of clarity, Helena turned to face Dr. Bastian. She knew that he was not there because of the belief she had a physical ailment; and although Helena felt like she was losing her grip on reality, she was not about to be sent to a mental hospital.

"Upset? No, I'm not upset Doctor. I am just tired that's all. Tired and a little down because I miss my husband and child." Helena responded in a slow, steady voice.

"What about the woman you told your mother you saw earlier? The one you said walked through the walls and into the street?" Dr. Bastian asked.

"That was just a dream I had, and when I awoke, I guess I was still a little spooked, but I know that it was all a dream." Helena lied trying to reassure Dr. Bastian that she was okay.

"Well, that sounds like it was a pretty disturbing dream, so I am going give you something to help calm your nerves and check on you again next week." Dr. Bastian offered while leaving some opium for Helena to take when needed.

"Thank you," Helena replied taking the medication from the Doctor's hands.

"Thank you so much for coming Doctor. I'll walk you out." Olivia said ushering Dr. Bastian to the door.

Once outside of Helena's room, Olivia asked the doctor about his diagnosis.

"Dr. Bastian, what's wrong with my daughter?" Olivia inquired.

"She seems to be suffering from depression, likely brought on by the separation from her husband and son. I think the opium should help, but you may want to try to engage her in activities to lift her spirits." Dr. Bastian answered.

"We never did throw a welcome home party for Helena; we thought her condition was too fragile, but now I think we should plan one. Maybe it will be just what she needs to bounce back. We would be pleased if you would join us, Doctor. I will send you an invitation once we make all of the arrangements." Olivia stated.

"That sounds like a wonderful idea Madam Marchand and thank you for the lovely invitation. I would be delighted to attend. It will also give me a chance to see if the treatment is working. Do send for me if her condition worsens." Dr. Bastian stated as he left.

Olivia bid Dr. Bastian farewell then asked one of the servants to bring Helena a glass of water. After the episode she witnessed earlier, Olivia wanted to get Helena started on treatment as soon as possible.

Helena took the opium. Soon after she drifted off to sleep and the medication held her nightmare at bay. Once Olivia checked on Helena and saw she was resting comfortably, she went to find her husband Alexander to bring him up to speed on the doctor's suggestion.

"The doctor just left," Olivia stated as she entered Alexander's study.

Alexander, who was just pouring himself an afternoon drink turned to face his wife.

"So, what did the good doctor say? Does he know what's wrong with our little girl?" Alexander asked as he nervously swirled the brown liquid around in his tumbler.

"He thinks that Helena is depressed because she misses John and John Jr," Olivia responded walking over to pour herself a glass as well.

Alexander stood astonished as his demure wife downed the harsh whiskey like it was apple juice.

"What's gotten into you Olivia, I have never seen you drink anything harder than a glass of red wine at one of our dinner parties or champagne at New Year's." Alexander proclaimed.

Putting down the tumbler and catching her breath, Olivia retorted "Well if you had seen our daughter scurrying about the room; running from an imaginary assailant, who she claimed, looked like a slave with soulless eyes and had the ability to walk through walls, you would understand why wine is not nearly enough."

"I thought the doctor told you she was only depressed over missing John and John Jr.?" Alexander quizzed.

"Well, that's because when Dr. Bastian came in to talk to Helena, she appeared calm and told him that she was merely upset over being separated from her family, which by the way, she never fully explained why she is here without them," Olivia replied.

"Do you think something happened between her and John?" Alexander asked.

"I think our daughter is not telling us the whole story about what happened in North Carolina. But right now, I am more concerned with trying to keep her from careening off the cliff of sanity; because darling, our little girl, is teetering on edge." Olivia answered.

"So, the doctor thinks a party is going to keep that from happening? Alexander questioned.

"That and the opium he prescribed," Olivia responded while showing Alexander the bottle.

"Well, I don't know if it will work, but I will try and do anything to help Helena" proclaimed Alexander.

"As will I. So, I guess I best get started with getting the plans together for this welcome home party." Olivia stated.

Alexander agreed and told Olivia to spare no expense. The cost was of no consequence to the Marchands; they were investing in their daughter's very sanity. No matter how improbable it was that a party would resolve the utter fear and erratic behavior Helena had displayed, her parents would do anything to bring their daughter back to them.

Helena's parents thought that perhaps throwing a massive party would be just the thing to boost their daughter's spirits. Helena didn't know this event would be the key to lifting more than her spirits, but Sarah's curse as well.

Chapter Five

Lady in Black

In the coming weeks, Helena's mood seemed to lighten, and she hadn't had any more hallucinations. Her parents were hopeful that she had finally snapped out of the psychotic state she had been in since coming back to New Orleans.

Dr. Bastian agreed to take her off the opium because it appeared her mood had stabilized. He also wanted the opportunity to observe her at the party without the influence of medication.

Two weeks had passed since Helena had stopped taking the medication and there had been no further incidents. Finally, the day of the party was upon them, and Helena had become excited about the idea. She had always loved a good party, mostly because it gave her an excuse to dress up and have everyone focus on her.

Helena was starting to feel like her old self again, selfish and self-centered. She had her parents spend a small fortune on the most lavish decorations, musical entertainment and of course the most exquisite gown for her re-entrance into New Orleans society.

"Sadie! Has my dress arrived yet?" Helena bellowed from her room upstairs. There was no immediate answer, so Helena became impatient.

"Where is that dumb slave?" She muttered to herself as she descended the stairs in search of Sadie. Even though slavery was abolished and Sadie came to work for the Marchands as a free Black years ago, Helena still viewed all the servants as nothing more than slaves.

"SADIE!" Helena shouted as she searched for her about the house.

Suddenly a middle-aged black woman with slightly graying hair and beautiful caramel colored skin appeared carrying Helena's dress.

"Yes, Miss Helena. I heard you bellowing from downstairs, but I was trying to finish pressing your dress for the party" Sadie said hurrying into the room.

"What took you so long? I could have made the dress myself by now!" Helena snapped.

Sadie stood looking Helena in the eye and said: "good then next time you can."

Snatching the dress from Sadie's hands, Helena angrily retorted "Well maybe you have outlived your usefulness!"

"Well, I see you are back to your normal charming self," Sadie replied sarcastically.

Helena replied "Very funny. Now leave me; I need to prepare for my party. I must be utterly ravishing, and this status of perfection takes time. I am going to get a little rest before the festivities begin; be sure to wake me before supper."

Sadie didn't reply as she turned and exited the room muttering to herself "No wonder you are losing your mind, you have been driving everyone else crazy for years!"

Helena had got comfortable that her nightmares were now behind her, and confident they would not return. In her arrogance, she returned to being her usual rude and malicious self. Readying herself for her grand debut, Helena tried on her dress and admired herself in the mirror.

"It's a perfect fit, and a perfect dress to return to my rightful place at the top of New Orleans' high society," Helena said out loud as she gazed at her reflection in shameless adoration.

Helena hung the perfectly tailored dress on the back of the door, satisfied that the gown was to her exact specifications. Preparation for the party and obtaining the perfect party dress had taken a lot out of her, so she laid down to take a nap. As Helena drifted off to sleep, she began to dream. It was a pleasant dream at first. She was at her party wearing her gown and looking flawless. All eyes were on her as she seemed to float about the room.

Helena enjoyed being the center of attention, but soon the focus of everyone in the room was directed at a mysterious guest who seemed to appear out of thin air. She was wearing a black dress, with her face covered by a black veil. When the woman lifted the veil, those expressions of admiration Helena saw in her guests' eyes were replaced with looks of horror. Helena turned to see what caught her guests' attention, and she was face to face with the woman who had been haunting her dreams since her return to New Orleans. The woman's skin looked like that of a decaying corpse, and her eyes were white and clouded over.

As Helena opened her mouth to scream, the woman suddenly reached out and started choking her. Helena woke up gasping, and although she heard herself cry out, no one heard her this time. She quickly tried to compose herself.

"Get ahold of yourself, Helena. It was just a dream. The woman isn't real" she said trying to calm down.

Helena got up and tried to pull herself together before getting ready for the party. She knew that Dr. Bastian was going to be there, and she was not going to give him any reason to think that she was losing her mind; even though Helena feared that she was.

Chapter Six

It's My Party, and I'll Die if I Want to

Helena took a warm bath with lavender water and tried to calm her rattled nerves. As she submerged herself in the sweet-smelling water, it appeared that her self-prescribed hydrotherapy treatment had done the trick. She had begun to relax and again turned her attention to preparing for her party.

After her bath, Helena dried off then dusted herself with sweet honey powder. Taking care to apply her makeup just right and pulling on her custom-made gown, Helena was finally ready to face her public. She fluffed her hair and blew herself an admiring kiss in the mirror, before heading downstairs.

Since Helena was the guest of honor, she thought it only proper that she be fashionably late to make an entrance. She descended the stairs in grand style with her emerald, green dress flowing behind her. It draped her flawless skin and accentuated her red hair and deep green eyes. As she reached the bottom of the stairs, she greeted her guests and eagerly received their plethora of compliments.

"Well Helena, it certainly is good to see you, Cher. You are just as beautiful as ever." Said a portly woman in an ostrich feathered dress that resembled a costume.

"Thank you, Mrs. Moreau. Oh my, that's an interesting gown you are wearing." Helena stated eyeing Mrs. Moreau's outfit and struggling not to laugh.

"You like it? It is supposed to be the latest fashion trend in Paris." Mrs. Moreau responded as she turned to show off her dress from all angles.

"No words could adequately describe how I feel about your dress, Mrs. Moreau. Do excuse me; I must greet my other guests. It was wonderful to see you again," Helena answered in a polite tone.

"Oh you are such a sweet child; forgive me for monopolizing all of your time. Go see to your other guests." Mrs. Moreau stated.

Helena bid Mrs. Moreau farewell and went to mingle. When she turned the corner, she saw a familiar face, her cousin Suzanne.

"Helena, how are you darling?" Suzanne said kissing Helena's cheeks.

"Well, I am just fabulous, how are you?" Helena replied, returning her cousin's affection.

"It has been years since I have seen you, where are your husband and son?" quizzed Suzanne.

Looking visibly uncomfortable, Helena tried to avoid the subject "oh they are still in North Carolina; I just came home for a little while to get away and see my parents."

Suzanne did not believe Helena's explanation and decided to probe deeper. "I have known you a long time Cher and I know when you are hiding something." She investigated.

"My dear sweet and annoyingly inquisitive cousin Suzanne, old age made you very suspicious; but I assure you there is nothing wrong." Helena retorted.

Suddenly the figure of a woman cloaked in all black caught Helena's eye, and she grew pale with terror.

"Oh Cher, you look as if you have seen a ghost. What is it?" Suzanne asked with genuine concern.

Remembering her cousin had dabbled in the unusual and had been known to frequent Soothsayers, Helena thought she might be able to help her figure out if she was haunted. Pulling Suzanne into another room, Helena began to tell her cousin all about the mysterious woman.

Once Helena had finished detailing all the strange things that she had endured since she had become a part of the Devereux family, Suzanne began to share her concern. She told Helena that she would take her to see a woman that lived in the Bayou and have her give Helena a reading. The thought that someone may be able to provide her with some answers to her dilemma, gave Helena the first sense of comfort she had in a while. She felt that she was now ready to continue to enjoy the rest of the evening.

When she and Suzanne rejoined the party, Helena saw that Dr. Bastian had arrived and was talking to her parents. Sensing that he was undoubtedly inquiring about her mental state, Helena thought it best to interject herself into the conversation.

"Dr. Bastian, it's nice to see that you made it out to celebrate with us tonight. How are you this evening?" Helena asked giving her best attempt to appear in perfect mental health.

"Helena, I was just thanking your lovely parents for their gracious invitation. I am doing quite well, but the real question is how are you doing? Have you experienced any further episodes since I took you off the opium?" Dr. Bastian inquired.

Nervously looking around in hopes that no one overheard the present conversation, Helena quickly replied. "Not a one. I have been sleeping like a baby."

"Well good, maybe all you needed was some long overdue rest. However, I would still like to see you in my office first thing in the morning." Dr. Bastian stated.

"Doctor, I hardly think that I need a visit; I am the picture of perfect mental health," Helena stated hoping she could rid herself of Dr. Bastian for good.

"Indulge me." Dr. Bastian replied with a smile.

"Ok then. I will see you first thing in the morning. Now if you will excuse me I have some old friends to whom I simply must say hello." Helena stated quickly putting as much distance between her and Dr. Bastian's prying eyes as possible.

Helena went to the library to get her bearings and saw the woman in black standing there as if she were waiting for her. It caught Helena so off guard she screamed before she could stop it. She watched in sheer terror as the figure appeared to float across the floor towards her, passing through furniture and anything else that was in her path. The scream had alerted some of the servants who were passing by from the kitchen, and they ran in to find a frantic Helena cowering in the corner.

"You ok miss?" Sadie asked searching the room for what could have possibly caused Helena to emit such a blood-curdling scream.

Helena leaped to her feet and grabbed Sadie. "You have to help me; she is going to kill me. I know it I just know it!" She pleaded now hiding behind Sadie.

"Who's gonna kill you, miss? There ain't nobody in here except us." Sadie said trying to calm Helena.

"Can't you see her? She is right there!" Helena screamed.

As Sadie was trying to convince Helena that no one else was in the room, the other servants had rushed to get her parents and Dr. Bastian. When they arrived, they saw a letter opener wielding Helena swatting at the air wildly to fend off her invisible attacker.

"I won't let you kill me!" Helena screamed at the air.

"Helena darling, who are you talking to?" Her father asked, but his questions fell on deaf ears. It was as if he were watching some horrifying nightmare play out in front of his eyes and he was helpless to stop it.

When Dr. Bastian's attempts to reason with Helena yielded no results, he instructed one of the servants to fetch his doctor's bag and two male servants to attempt to restrain her. She turned the letter opener on them, and Dr. Bastian in attempts to ward them off as well. They managed to subdue her long enough for Dr. Bastian to inject her with a sedative. At that point, it did not take much convincing for her parents to sign her over to Dr. Bastian's care and commit her to the New Orleans City Insane Asylum for evaluation.

Once the sedative had taken effect, Helena was carried to her room and restrained until Dr. Bastian could arrange transport to the hospital in the morning. He assured her parents that she would receive the best possible care but also informed them that this was just the first part of the process. If she were found to need further treatment, they would transfer Helena to the East Louisiana State Hospital for the Insane.

The New Orleans City Insane Asylum was established in 1854 by the New Orleans City Council. The Council also gave "Recorders" like Dr. Bastian, of various Districts the power to commit patients to the asylum for evaluation until they could transport them to the state hospital in Jackson. During this period the criteria to be considered "insane" and locked away for an extended period was minuscule at best.

Asylums that were built to house hundreds became homes or tombs for thousands. The overcrowed conditions were based solely on the ignorance of what constituted mental illness; and the non-existence of humane and effective treatments for those who were suffering from it. With Helena having active hallucinations and being a woman during this period, becoming committed to an asylum for any length of time did not bode a favorable outcome, even for a Marchand.

Chapter Seven

What's in a Name?

The next morning dawned with a beautiful sunrise. Helena awoke feeling rested with the morning sun planting warm kisses on her face, and the birds serenading her with their sweet songs. She laid there taking in the ambiance of the morning and thinking that this was going to be a beautiful day. Helena was going to put last night's horrible chain of events behind her and go with her cousin to see the soothsayer in the bayou. Finally, she was going to get some answers and resolution to her ongoing nightmare.

A strand of Helena's long red hair was lying on her face and tickling her nose. When she attempted to remove it, she realized that she was immobile. Helena first thought was that she was still asleep and having one of those horrible nightmares that were accompanied by sleep paralysis, but soon she discovered it was much worse. She was wide awake, but her arms were restrained.

As Helena started screaming and struggling to free herself, her parents entered the room with Dr. Bastian close behind.

"Good morning Helena. How are you feeling this morning?" Dr. Bastian asked watching as Helena continued to thrash about her bed like a fish out of water.

Falling to her bed exhausted from struggling, Helena blew the menacing curl of hair from her face and retorted "Aside from waking up finding myself strapped to my bed, I'm fabulous. How are you this marvelous morning?"

"Now I know this is a little disconcerting..." Dr. Bastian started attempting to lessen the apparent gravity of the situation.

"Disconcerting?" Helena laughed interrupting Dr. Bastian. "Is that what this is? Why thank you, Doctor, for that simplistic explanation for how it feels to awake from your sleep; and find that you are bound like a goddamn mummy!"

"Helena darling, it was for your protection" Olivia interjected.

Whipping her head around to face her parents Helena quizzed "Protection? Tying me up is how you protect me? Daddy, how could you let them do this to me? I would have expected this treatment from mother, she never understood or supported me, but you daddy? I am your little girl."

Olivia stood with her mouth open with visible shock and hurt feelings over Helena's remarks, but she didn't speak. Her father Alexander attempted to move to comfort his daughter, but Helena turned her head. Soon more figures appeared in the doorway wearing white.

"Who are they?" Helena asked eerily calm.

Turning to look at the men, Dr. Bastian responded: "They are here to help me with your transport."

"What transport? Where are you taking me?" Helena asked now heavily breathing as she realizes what is about to happen.

"To the New Orleans City Asylum, your parents have signed you over to my care, and it is my recommendation that you be placed there for evaluation. It is just so the city physician can look at you and prescribe the best treatment for you. Nothing to worry about, you are in good hands" assured Dr. Bastian.

Helena began to struggle again to free herself from her restraints and started screaming. Dr. Bastian was prepared because he anticipated she would not go without a fight. He sedated Helena, and once she was asleep, he instructed the men to load her into the carriage for transport.

Sadie and her 8-year-old granddaughter Cleo stood with the other servants as they watched them carry Helena away. Everyone agreed that something was seriously wrong with Helena, but only Sadie knew what it was. Helena was hexed.

Helena was taken to the New Orleans City Asylum as promised, but her evaluation was little more than Dr. Bastian relaying what he witnessed at the party to the city physician and his transferring Helena to Jackson. Helena's parents were not allowed to visit her at the city asylum. The staff told them once she settled in at the state asylum, they could see her.

The Marchands reluctantly agreed. They filled her cousin Suzanne in on the details when she arrived at the plantation to get Helena that morning. Suzanne was taking Helena to see the woman in the Bayou, but since she couldn't, she decided to go anyway and see if the lady could still help her cousin.

All of this occurred with Helena restrained in the city asylum under constant sedation. Days had passed, but to Helena, it seemed like only hours had gone by since Dr. Bastian first removed her from her home. The first time she could remain awake, she was transferred to Jackson.

When Helena awoke, she found herself in the same restraints, but she was no longer in the comforts of her elegant plantation home. Now the bright sunny yellow walls to which she usually awoke, were replaced with those that were dingy white and lifeless. Her soft feather bed was now a hard cot, and her abode of solitude was now an overcrowded habitat for the indigent and the insane.

Helena wanted to scream, but she feared that if she did they would just sedate her again and she wouldn't get to talk to whoever was in charge. She needed to let them know that this was all one big misunderstanding and that she didn't belong there. Helena waited and waited, but no one came. She laid in bed for hours with no one to check on her.

Countless times in the past, Helena had berated poor Sadie for breaching her sacred space to inquire if there was anything that she needed. But there was no Sadie there; and no area that was sacred. Helena attempted to plead her case to anyone who would hear her, but her only confidants were her fellow patients; and no matter what their level of understanding or empathy, they were just as powerless as she was in there. The staff was so overworked that they didn't have time to attend to her needs, nor the desire to listen to her pleas.

All attempts to communicate her station and place in society fell on deaf ears. For the first time in Helena's life, no one bowed to her wishes nor placed her on a pedestal. Inside those walls, she was on the same level as those she viewed as less than human; and subjected to the same treatment.

There were no gourmet meals served at her leisure, and no baths in lavender water. Here the meals were barely edible, and bathing was infrequent at best. It was much more common for staff to dunk patients in freezing tubs of ice water, to snap them out of their depressed states.

The hell and atrocities that occurred behind these walls in the name of science rivaled any medieval torture chamber. Helena was about to witness and experience firsthand, the level of torment that she had levied against so many slaves on the Marchand plantation.

The asylum was massive and self-contained; the staff used patients for a variety of purposes as part of their "treatment." They were tortured and sometimes killed by the latest in misguided revolutionary treatments. They were also used as labor to work the massive acres of farmland. Patients were the new legal form of slaves and Helena was no exception.

Once you were committed to the state asylum names were irrelevant, even the name Marchand. In here, a patient by any name is still insane.

Chapter Eight

A Black War Hero, Ain't Nothing but a Dead Nigger

Winter 1866

Once Peter had gotten word that John and his family made it safely to their new Canadian home, he could finally focus on the matters in North Carolina. There were some dark days in the wake of the Civil War, and Peter was happy it ended without any further losses to his family.

Peter had come to love Thomas and Jacob as if they were his sons, so losing Thomas in the war not only devastated Thomas' wife Marie and son TJ but every other member of the family as well.

Peter rejoiced along with Jacob's parents Sarah and Nathaniel when he learned that Jacob was to return from the war unharmed. Sarah and her husband Nathaniel had remained on the Devereux plantation as house servants after the war freed them, but Peter embraced them as a family.

After the war ended, things died down a little, and Sarah was able to enjoy reconnecting with her husband and counting her blessings. Their son Jacob

47

was returning safely from the war, and their daughter Marie and their grandchildren had arrived safely in Canada. Sarah and Nathaniel had even talked about maybe one day joining them there.

When Jacob came home from the war, he wasn't sure exactly what he was going to do with his life, but Jacob knew that he wasn't going to do it in North Carolina. He loved his family, and although he wanted to soak up as much time with them as possible, he knew his ambitions would not be fulfilled or appreciated there. He also knew that as soon as the locals found out that he fought with the Union, his very life is endangered.

Jacob was coming home the way he said he would, as a free man and a war hero. Jacob was proud to have been a part of the fight for freedom for Blacks. However, when he crossed the North Carolina line, Jacob felt a mixture of emotions. Jacob was excited to see his family and to have them see him in his uniform, but he was sad that his brother-in-law Thomas was not coming home with him.

Thomas gave his life to protect him on the battlefield and for that, Jacob had to bear the guilt that his sister would never hold her husband again; and his nephew would never grow up with his father in his life. There was a myriad of feelings coursing through Jacob's body at once, but the one feeling that grew strongest as the train approached its destination was the sense of overwhelming dread.

Jacob knew that coming home as a civil war hero could be more dangerous than fighting the war itself. As the train pulled into the station, Jacob tried to shake those thoughts out of his head and gathered his things. As he stepped onto the station platform, he saw two familiar faces staring at him, but they were not friendly.

Billy and Bobby McAllister were two of the most racist men Jacob had ever met. They were confederate sympathizers, and both had sons that fought in the war as confederate soldiers. The brothers and their sons lynched any Blacks that had the unfortunate luck to get caught in their path. When Jacob attempted to pass, he was careful not to make eye contact, but that didn't matter to the McAllisters.

"Excuse me," Jacob said as he passed by the brothers.

When they saw the uniform Jacob was wearing; it made him an instant target. There was nothing that Jacob could do to avoid what he felt in the pit of his stomach coming. The hairs on the back of his neck stood on end as Jacob heard Bobby McAllister say "'Scuse ya? Dere ain't no 'scuse fo ya boy!" then shoved Jacob as he walked passed them.

Then turning his attention to his brother, he asked: "Billy did ya hear whut dis uppity nigger jus said?"

"I sure did Bobby. He thank dat dere uny-fom makes'em sum kinda hero!" Billy said with a laugh.

Joining his brother in mocking Jacob, Bobby responded "Our boys; now dey is heroes. Dey blew the faces off pleny of Black coons durin da war!

Somebody shoulda told 'em dat 'round heh, a Black war hero ain't nuthin but a dead nigger."

Jacob stared at the two brothers in their eyes and didn't flinch. He had fought bravely for his country and his freedom. Jacob didn't back down from an army of confederate soldiers, and he was not going to back down from two confederate sympathizers. In that very moment, Jacob decided he would rather die on his feet as a man, than live on his knees like a slave.

When they couldn't instill the fear in Jacob they had hoped, the brothers became infuriated, and they lunged for Jacob. Although the brothers were known for being violent, neither of them had any real fighting skills. As a result, their plan to have some fun "putting Jacob in his place" didn't go well. Each time one of them swung, Jacob dodged their punches but landed several of his own, which increased the brothers' anger. When it was clear they were not going to win this battle; they decided that it was best to save this fight for later.

"Ya gon die ta'night nigger! I ain't gonna fo'get dis! Ya, hear me, nigger?" Billy shouted as he wiped the blood from his lip.

Their pride was wounded and for that Jacob was sentenced in their minds to pay the ultimate price. The brothers backed away from Jacob, but everyone, including those who witnessed the scuffle, knew that Jacob was a dead man walking. His notion that he could defend himself against two White men had just signed his death warrant.

Jacob knew that he had won the battle, but the war was not over. He hurried to make his way home and caught a ride part of the way with some Black sharecroppers he met on the road. They had seen the incident that had just happened and knew it wouldn't be safe for Jacob to try to walk. It was going to be dark soon, and no Black person wanted to be caught walking the roads at night.

"Git up heh son, I tek ya home. Dem medas on ya ches' ain't gon hep nun ifin dem boys catch ya on da roid" an old Black man said offering Jacob a ride.

"Thank you, sir," Jacob said climbing into the wagon.

"Whey ya goin son?" the old man asked.

"The Devereux plantation sir" Jacob responded.

"Debero? Peta Debero? Dats one'a da richest men in town. He yo Massa?" The old man quizzed.

Jacob looked stunned but politely replied "I have no master. I am a free man sir, not a slave."

The old man turned and looked at Jacob with a look of concern and stated. "Don't let dem medas on yo chess fool ya son. We ain't free. Da law say we ain't slaves, but dey still don't say we men. Jus 'cuz dey let ya wear dat uni'fom don' mean dey won't hang ya in it."

Jacob sat in silence the rest of the trip, as he thought about what the old man had said. When they arrived, the man stopped at the end of the road.

"Dis is as fa as I go, son. Lik I say, no Black man wanna get caught out on dese roids at night; and I gots a ways ta go fo I gets home mysef." The old man stated bidding Jacob farewell.

"Thank you for the ride, sir; you be safe out there," Jacob said.

"Don ya worry bout me son, Ya just keep yo eyes open, dem boys ain't gonna fo'get whut happ'n ta'day; and ya can be sho dey comin ta'night." The old man warned.

Jacob nodded as the old man drove away. Nathaniel was out in the yard finishing up some gardening when he saw Jacob coming up the road. Nathaniel wiped the sweat from his brow to make sure he didn't see things. When he saw it was Jacob, he jumped for joy.

"Hummingbird! Come on out heh woman and see who don come home!" Nathaniel shouted.

"What are you yelling 'bout Nate?" Sarah asked as she came out of the house, with Peter close behind.

When Sarah looked out and saw Jacob coming down the road, she screamed and ran to meet him.

"Oh, sweet Jesus, my baby done come home," Sarah shouted as she ran.

When she reached Jacob, she threw her arms around him and hugged him like she was never going to let go. Once Sarah finally released her grip, Nathaniel and Peter got a chance to get a hug in as well.

"OOOO WEEEE, look at dem medas hummingbird; our son is a real war hero!" Nathaniel said before hugging his son so tight he lifted him off the ground.

Laughing, Peter said "The man survived the war, don't kill'em now" as he went to hug Jacob as well.

The comment, though innocent, made Jacob reflect on what had happened earlier and the old man's warning. Once Peter gave him a heartfelt embrace he pulled Jacob away from him to get a good look at him in his uniform. When he did, he noticed a strange look on Jacob's face, which instantly faded the smile from his own.

"What's the matter, son?" Peter asked sensing something was very wrong.

The question filled Jacob's parents with concern, and they came close to hear the answer. Jacob didn't want to ruin his homecoming by recounting his earlier incident, but he also knew he didn't want to put his family's life in danger either, so he told them.

As they listened to Jacob tell them about his run-in with the McAllister brothers, Sarah's blood ran cold. She knew that embarrassing two White men, by besting them in a fight was not going to go without consequence. They would come for her son; and they would not come to fight, they would come to kill.

Sarah drifted off in her mind for a moment. She saw Jacob's lips moving, but her mind was no longer processing his words. Sarah envisioned her son hanging from a tree for the unforgivable crime of being a Black man. There was no way that Sarah was going to let that happen; she would hang in his place first.

Sarah came back into the conversation and heard Peter say, "Don't you worry son, I'm not losing another member of this family."

He looked at Sarah in her eyes to reassure her that he was not about to let anything happen to Jacob, but that was a mutual promise. Sarah had already started thinking about what she was going to do about their expected yet unwelcomed visitors. She swore on her life, if they came for Jacob, she would go for them.

Chapter Nine

If You Mess with a Bull, You Get the Horns
If You Mess with a Mother, You Die

Sarah went upstairs to get Jacob's room ready so that he could rest. She figured he was probably tired from his journey and his earlier encounter. As she made up his bed, she dashed some lavender water mixed with some of her unique herbs on his pillow to help him rest. Then went back downstairs to prepare dinner.

While Jacob was upstairs resting, Sarah, Nathaniel, and Peter were in the kitchen working on how they were going to handle the McAllister brothers. Over the years, Sarah had filled Nathaniel in on her unique abilities; as well as what she had done to those who had crossed her and threatened her family. Now that he was up to speed, he wasn't worried about the McAllister brothers; but they most certainly should be worried about Sarah.

"What's da plan Hummingbird? Nathaniel asked.

"There's always room in the pond. It served as quite the suitable accommodations for old Winston years ago." Peter quipped.

With a sinister smirk, Sarah replied "We wouldn't want anyone to start to question why dead bodies keep popping up on our property. As much as I would love to watch those animals sink to their watery grave, we must be smart. Besides, I have something much more fitting in store for these two."

Peter and Nathaniel listened closely while Sarah divulged her plan. When everyone knew what to do, Sarah left to go to her room and make the things she needed for her spells. Sarah first concocted a protection spell for Jacob using some strands of his hair. And then took one of Thomas' insignias Jacob sent home when Thomas died in battle. She would use this for her ultimate revenge.

Once everything was in place, she called Jacob down for dinner. Everyone sat at the table in front of a lavish feast Sarah prepared to celebrate her son's return home. Peter gave thanks for his family and prayed for their protection. They ate, drank and filled each other in on all that had transpired since they had been apart. Jacob entertained his family with stories from his time in the Army, and they told him about what was happening there at home and about Marie and John fleeing to Canada with the kids.

They were so engrossed in the happiness of being together; they had almost forgotten about the impending danger. It didn't take long for the family to remember. The family's long-awaited reunion was interrupted by the sound of glass breaking. When they rushed to the front of the house, they saw a brick thrown through the front window. Through the broken glass, they saw bright flames from torches lighting up the night sky like the sun.

Peter opened the door and went out on the front porch. Sarah, Jacob, and Nathaniel went around to the back of the house then went out into the woods to wait.

The McAllister brothers were sitting on horseback along with their two sons, one of which was pulling a cart behind his horse. All the men were wearing hoods over their faces made from feed sacks, and the sons were each wearing their confederate uniforms. Peter stepped onto the porch with his shotgun cocked and pointed straight at Bobby McAllister's head.

"Well, I hate to break it to you boys, but you are a little early for Halloween, and those costumes are not very original," Peter stated with a smirk.

"We ain't got no issue wit ya Mr. Devereux. Jus give us da nigger, and nobody else'll get hurt." Billy McAllister stated from behind his mask.

"Nigger? I don't know what kind of candy that is, but I am sure we don't have any niggers here. In fact, if that is you behind that ridiculous feed sack mask, Billy McAllister, candy is the last thing you need with those rotten teeth. By the way, you may want to inform your companions that the South lost, so wearing that uniform just looks like they are sore losers." Peter quipped.

"Now I don't wanna have ta shoot ya Mr. Devereux, but we ain't leaving here without that nigger," Billy shouted.

"Well, I guess your brother will be leaving here without his head, considering I have this shotgun aimed right at it. I know it's covered by a sack, but it's so extraordinarily large that I am sure a blind man could hit it from this distance." Peter warned.

"Look, Mr. Devereux; it is my God given right ta smite down any nigger that dares ta fo'get his place! We came for justice!" Billy shouted.

Peter lowered his rifle and replied, "then justice is served."

Suddenly, Billy felt a sharp prick followed by being very dizzy. Within seconds he was unconscious. The men were so preoccupied with looking at Peter, they were not paying attention to their surroundings, and their feed sac masks drastically limited their line of sight. One by one, the men had all been pricked by darts dipped in devil's snare, a robust plant that had strong hallucinogenic properties. The brothers had loaded their cart with rope, tar and other items with which they intended to torture Jacob. Unbeknownst to them, those items would be their own demise.

Peter loaded the men onto the cart with the help of some of the sharecroppers on his land. He then took them deep into the woods, far away from the Devereux plantation to meet Sarah, Nathaniel, and Jacob. When the men awoke, they were all propped against a tree. They could not move, even though nothing was holding them. Peter removed each of the men's masks.

"Wake up sunshine, its justice time." Peter sang as he looked at the men's now horrified faces.

"Now I thought about what you said, and I agree. When someone has been wronged, then justice should be served. Jacob, would you come here a minute son?" Peter said motioning for Jacob.

When Jacob was standing in front of the men, Peter continued. "Now Jacob here is like a son to me. I know you haven't had the pleasure to know anything about me because we don't belong to the same social circles. So, let me give you a crash course. I am the most ruthless son of a bitch you will ever meet. When it comes to my family, there is no limit to the amount of hell I will bring to anyone who threatens them. Unfortunately for you, I am nothing compared to his actual parents." Peter said with a smirk.

"I hear you boys have a problem with a Black man in uniform, so I invited some of my friends to this little JUSTICE party," Sarah said with a sinister smile.

There was an eerie sound of trees rustling and twigs breaking. The men watched in terror as two negro soldiers moved towards them. The closer they got, they noticed that these soldiers had eyes that were white and clouded and skin that looked as if it was decomposing. The brothers were still under the power of the devil's snare, so Sarah used a little power of suggestion to guide them into a full-fledged nightmare.

The men tried to move, but they couldn't; they also could not speak. Sarah walked over to them and blew a white powder in their faces; then told each of them that their sons were the enemy, and when she commanded them they were to exact their revenge. Although they were conscious of what was happening to them, they had no control to stop it. The men watched in horror as the dead soldiers walked right into them, melting into their bodies. Once they were possessed by the spirit of the dead soldiers, each man left the woods to carry out Sarah's command.

That night both brothers returned home with no memory of what happened and went to bed, but they were about to experience first-hand the pain they had inflicted on so many families. When Sarah spoke the words "ce que vous avez prévu pour mon fils, vous ferez la vôtre. What you had planned for my son, you will do to yours." Each possessed man rose from their beds and went to their son's room, dragging them out of bed and out the door. Their wives woke to the sounds of their husbands torturing and killing their sons right before their eyes.

Billy McAllister hung his son on their front lawn and set his body on fire. Bobby McAllister tied his son to a tree and poured hot tar over his body. The brothers were forced to endure the torture of not only watching their loved ones suffer the same fate as their past victims, but committing those acts themselves with no control to stop it.

When it was over, the men woke to see what they had done. The pain and guilt washed over them like a flood. They were both arrested and charged with murder. Bobby tried to take his own life but was unsuccessful. Death would have been a release, but he was denied even that.

When they told the judge that a spirit possessed their bodies and made them slaughter their sons, they were deemed insane. Each man was sentenced to spend the rest of their lives in the state's psychiatric hospital.

Although the McAllister brothers were no longer a threat, Peter knew it was dangerous for a Black man to travel anywhere in the south during that time; especially if the man had also been a union soldier in the Civil War.

Peter wasn't about to risk Jacob being lynched by some fervent ex-plantation owner after surviving a war; so, he arranged for Jacob to receive the same safe passage he had for John and his family. Jacob remained at home with his family just long enough for Peter to arrange his trip to Canada. He contacted the old minister that had helped Marie and John relocate there with their family. He gave Jacob a nice sum of money to help him get set up in Canada and Marie's address.

Jacob's run-in with the McAllister brothers cut his visit home a lot shorter than he intended. It also introduced North Carolina's rural society to the more primal side of Peter Devereux. Peter's ruthlessness and protective nature when it came to his family were legendary in New Orleans, but since moving to Tobacco Road, he had tried to keep a more dignified profile. He didn't want to attract too much attention to their secrets, but when someone threatened his family, all bets were off. Sarah and Nathaniel were sad to see their son leave again, but they knew it was still too dangerous for him to stay.

The war had officially ended the institution of slavery, but it had not stopped the hatred and violence against Blacks in the United States. Now that Jacob was leaving for Canada, it made Peter think about his son being there as well. Peter knew that although he hated his son and grandchildren being so far away, their lives were in danger every day they had remained in North Carolina. He took comfort in the fact that John and Marie were finally in a place they could honestly be together, happy and free. Now, Jacob would be there as well. Like Sarah and Nathaniel, Peter contemplated going to Canada to see his family one day. In fact, Peter had a feeling one day they all would bid farewell to Tobacco Road.

In Their Shoes

1874

When Helena arrived at the hospital, the Marchands had repeatedly tried to see her; but the charismatic Dr. Bastian assured them that she was responding well to the new treatments that he was working on with her, but any reminders of her home could set her back. The Marchands reluctantly agreed in the beginning, but then they grew tired of waiting and wanted to see for themselves.

Dr. Bastian agreed to the Marchands visit but made sure that when they saw Helena, she was well-groomed, and their appointment occurred in a room reserved for just such an occasion. It was brightly lit and colorful; it had lovely paintings on the wall and beautiful fresh cut flowers about the place.

It gave the Marchands the impression that Helena was receiving great care, and Dr. Bastian made sure that Helena was too high on opiates to tell them otherwise. Satisfied that Dr. Bastian was taking care of their daughter, they didn't question him again and followed his instructions with no contact.

Once Dr. Bastian was sure that he had the Marchands out of his hair, he could focus on Helena's treatment.   Dr. Bastian tried several techniques to rid Helena of her psychosis in between keeping her in an opiate-induced state. Before long the months had turned into years, and each passed in a haze like fog of nightmarish visions and drug-induced daydreams.

When Helena arrived there were only a little over 100 residents; now there were over 600. The increase in numbers had taken its toll on the asylum's amenities and staff. The facility was in bad shape with monies now lacking for patient's clothing and other necessities. A new superintendent and Jackson native, Dr. John Welch Jones had recently taken over operations, delving into his funds for the first three months to keep the facility running.

As a more permanent and lucrative option to fund operations, Dr. Welch began teaching patients how to make bricks to continue to expand the asylum. He also organized patients as farm laborers to produce vegetables for consumption within the hospital; a fact Helena was about to learn firsthand.

"And how are we feeling today?" Dr. Bastian asked as he entered Helena's room.

Holding up her restrained arms, Helena coolly responded "Oh I don't know. How do you think I am doing doctor? I have been chained to this bed like an animal so long I don't even know what day it is."

With a smug grin, Dr. Bastian replied "Well that is all about to change today. You are going to be allowed to get some fresh air and exercise. I believe this will go a long way in clearing your mind of those disturbing visions."

An excited Helena eagerly agreed that being allowed to be removed from the restraints would be helpful in her recovery. An orderly came in and assisted with removing Helena's constraints and gave her clothing to wear outside.

Noticing the wardrobe choice Helena quizzed "Where exactly am I supposed to be going wearing these rags?"

With feigned offense, Dr. Bastian placed his hand on his chest and replied: "I wouldn't want you to sully any of your expensive frocks during your exercise regimen."

"What am I supposed to be doing? I was thinking a leisurely walk about the garden should be good enough to start" Helena offered still feeling that her station should afford her the choice in what she does.

"I am so glad you have an interest in seeing the garden because that is exactly the location I had in mind for you to get your exercise! Now if you will kindly follow Nurse Smith, she will escort you outside" Dr. Bastian stated.

Nurse Smith led Helena out to the garden where she noticed patients weeding the ground in preparation to plant seeds. When the nurse handed her a garden hoe, Helena looked at the nurse as if she needed to be a patient herself.

"Why on earth are you handing me that thing? I am here to walk amongst the garden for my exercise, not work it like a slave!" Helena barked

"Oh, I am so sorry for the misunderstanding, miss. " Nurse Smith replied: with feigned humility,

Feeling that she had put the nurse in her place, she replied: "That is quite alright I realize someone of your limited breeding may be easily confused about what a socialite does."

With a smirk, Nurse Smith replied "Oh you misunderstand miss. I am not sorry for that. I am sorry that you still have not realized your name is of no consequence in here. I guess it's your limited life experience that makes you easily confused about what state property does."

Nurse Smith handed Helena the hoe again and walked away. A young Black woman walked over to her to show her how to till the soil.

"Heh let me show ya how it don," the girl said taking the hoe from Helena and breaking up the soil. Still standing in disbelief, Helena said softly, "but I'm a Marchand, I have never had to work the grounds; that is why we had slaves. The dirt of the fields never sullied my shoes."

The young girl stopped working for a brief second and looked up at Helena and said: "Weh I guess ya gon see wha it feel lak ta walk in dey shoes." Then she handed the hoe back to Helena and went back to tending her work.

Helena stood there motionless, as the feeling of utter shame and disgrace enveloped her body. Being reduced to the same level as a field hand was more torturous to her than any experimental treatment she had endured during her entire stay at the asylum.

The years and the degradation of her experiences at the asylum were slowly taking a toll on her. Helena feared that if she weren't crazy when they admitted her, she would surely lose her mind if not soon released.

Surrendering to her current state, Helena watched the other patients turn the soil. She had no idea what she was supposed to do, but Helena knew that she was not going to be able to survive in here alone anymore. Swallowing her pride, Helena humbly went over to the young girl who had offered her help earlier.

"Hello. My name is Helena. I'm sorry about before. It is taking me some time to get used to being in here. I am not sure what I am supposed to do, so I would be very grateful if you would help me." Helena said with eyes cast down.

The young girl stood wiping her hands on her dress before extending it to Helena. "Min Abina. Ya can call meh Abby."

Helena stared at the young girl's hand and finally shook it reluctantly. As she watched the girl continue the gardening lesson she had begun earlier, Helena finally hit her rock bottom and saw this as a sign she would never leave these grounds alive. As Helena let that thought wash over her like a tide, she began to sink into a feeling of overwhelming dread.

Mimicking the actions of the other patients in the garden, Helena performed manual labor for the first time in her life. She quickly realized it was no easy task. Her body and hands began to ache, but there was no end to her workday in sight. She suddenly thought that this must be what it feels like to be a slave. The thought alone filled her with immeasurable sadness, and her body began to shake violently from crying, but no one came to console her. Helena was left to till the soil and water it with her tears.

Strange Magic

When Helena's cousin Suzanne arrived at the Marchand plantation on that fateful day years ago, she was too late. Helena's strange behavior had caused her desperate parents to sign her over to the care of Dr. Bastian, who did not allow anyone to visit Helena for the first year of her commitment. Still, Suzanne went to visit the old lady in the Bayou to see if she could help her cousin.

The old lady told Suzanne it appeared that someone had been working spells on her cousin, but she needed a strand of her hair pulled from the root to be sure, which proved very difficult given Dr. Bastian's ban on visitation. Even when he lifted the visitation ban slightly, there was strict supervision. It would be years before Suzanne managed to get close enough to her cousin to get the strand of hair she needed on one of those visits.

Once Suzanne managed to get the strand of hair and return to the Bayou, sadly the old woman had died. She asked if there was someone else who could help her but given Helena's reputation for the treatment of slaves and servants, no one readily volunteered.

Feeling hopeless Suzanne returned to the Marchand plantation. She walked into Helena's room and looked around. The Marchands had not changed a thing. They wanted Helena's place to be exactly the way she left it when she returned. It was their way of keeping hope alive that she would one day came home to them. Picking up a photograph of her and Helena as children, Suzanne began to cry.

"I am so sorry I couldn't help you Helena," Suzanne said aloud looking at the picture. "I went to see the old woman that day, and she was certain she could help. All she needed was a strand of your hair from the root. A simple request really, but that Dr. Bastian wouldn't let me see you. And by the time I had the chance to retrieve what the old woman needed, she had since passed on. I have tried all I could to find someone to help me my dear cousin but to no avail. I fear no one can help us now". Suzanne cried clutching the picture. She was so distraught that she did not notice that someone was standing in the doorway.

"I can help you miss." a voice said from the doorway.

Suzanne jumped to her feet, startled that someone overheard her conversation. "Jesus Christ girl, you almost gave me a heart attack! Don't you know it is not polite to listen to others' private thoughts? Who are you anyway?" Suzanne quizzed.

"Sorry miss didn't mean to scare you. I'm Sadie's granddaughter Cleo, and I'm tasked to clean

Miss Helena's room every day. Mrs. Marchand wants to make sho it's nice and fresh for when Miss Helena come home, and she never 'lows no one ta come in here less they are cleaning. And since I'm da only one who clean dis room, I thought it strange ta hear a voice coming from it. When I came in, I heard you talking 'bout da old woman in the Bayou." Cleo said.

"What do you know about her? Suzanne asked wiping away her tears.

"I know that she was very powerful, but not as powerful as my grandma Sadie" Cleo replied

With a look mixed with surprise and hope, Suzanne grabbed Cleo by the arms and pleaded "Cleo you have to take me to Sadie at once. She may be the only hope to save Helena!"

Cleo complied and took Suzanne to find Sadie, who was outside sweeping the front porch. Sadie was none too happy to learn that her overzealous granddaughter had spilled a secret that she had kept from the Marchands for years.

Sadie never wanted them to know just what she was capable of; however, Suzanne had always been kind to her and treated with respect. She had raised both Helena and Suzanne alongside her son Solomon, who was Cleo's father. Unlike Suzanne, Helena held no gratitude for that.

Sadie had noticed what was going on with Helena from the very beginning but felt no urgency in trying to relieve her suffering. As far as she was concerned, that misery couldn't have happened to a better person. It was only her fondness for Suzanne that persuaded Sadie to help Helena. Sadie told Suzanne that she would help her, but that she couldn't breathe a word to the Marchands. Suzanne agreed, and Sadie told her to meet her in her room later that night and bring the strand of Helena's hair.

That night, Suzanne crept up the stairs to the attic where Sadie slept. She knocked softly on the door to alert Sadie that she had arrived. Sadie opened the door and beckoned Suzanne inside.

"Come on in here child and close the door'. Sadie said.

Suzanne did as she was instructed, checking to make sure no one saw her come in. Once inside, Suzanne saw a single candle lit the room, and a small tin lay beside it. On the other side of the tin was a pile of small bones. Suzanne was a little frightened that someone she had known all her life was said to be a powerful mambo.

"You got Miss Helena's hair?" Sadie asked

Suzanne pulled the strand of long red hair from a small pouch and handed it to Sadie with no words. Then she sat in amazement as she watched Sadie start chanting some phrase and place Helena's hair in the tin. She poured some oil over it and lit it with the flame from the candle.

As the strand burned, Sadie picked up the small bones and shook them in her hand. She then blew on them once and dropped them back on the table. As Sadie inspected how the bones fell, a disturbing look came over her face. The look made Suzanne's blood run cold as she inquired about what Sadie saw.

"What is it, Sadie? Can you tell what happened to Helena?" Suzanne quizzed nervously.

Sadie slowly sat back from the table and looked at Suzanne. "Sho can. Miss Helena done crossed the wrong witch."

"You know who put a spell on Helena? Can you tell what it was?" Suzanne asked.

"Naw, don't know who she crossed. But I know dey powerful, even more, powerful than me!" Sadie said.

Suzanne suddenly felt that her cousin's actions and treatment of people, especially negro people had finally caught up with her. Now the question was could and would someone help to save her.

"What did they do to her Sadie?" Suzanne asked.

Looking back at the bones, Sadie replied "Dey hexed her with a powerful spell. One that gives the caster control over her thoughts. The caster can make Miss Helena see thangs and even control her dreams. The spell is an old one; it's been on her for some time now. It has worked its way into her very soul. They bound together, and the only way to free her is to break the bond.

"Can you break it? I will make sure you are rewarded for your kindness if you help Helena." Suzanne offered.

Taking a deep breath, Sadie thought for a minute about whether she should help the woman who deserved every ounce of the punishment she was receiving. Finally, she agreed to help.

"Yeah, I can. But I need some thangs first so, I will do it tomorrow under da full moon. That's when I will have the power to break it. But you must be careful. Once the tie is broken, the mambo that cast it gonna know and that may put Miss Helena in more danger" Sadie warned.

"I'll be careful. Just please help my cousin" Suzanne pleaded.

"Alright then. When the moon is done, and the sun rises the next mo'nin, that tie will be broke, and Helena will be free." Sadie assured.

Suzanne hugged Sadie with tears in her eyes and re-confirmed her promise to keep Sadie's secret. Then she went back to the guest room to sleep. As promised Sadie gathered all she needed to break the spell on Helena, but to destroy this hex, she was going to need some help from someone more powerful than she was. Sadie put all the ingredients in a bag, grabbed Cleo and set off to the bayou to see her family.

Sadie walked through the dark swamp lands and took a little boat to her family's home on the bayou. When she came to the small house, she saw her father sitting outside smoking a pipe.

"Oh, my ole weary eyes must be playing tricks on me! Is that my prodigal daughter returning to the fold?" Obataye quizzed.

"I was never reckless Papa," Sadie said approaching her father.

"No? What do you call throwing away such a powerful gift?" Obataye asked

"I didn't throw it away Papa. I just wanted a different life." Sadie answered.

"Humph, a life with your family full of power and respect wasn't good enough of a life for you. So, what brings you here now? And who is this girl you bring with you?" Obataye inquired.

"I need your help to break a spell; and this is your great-granddaughter Cleopatra, but we call her Cleo." Replied Sadie.

"Spell? Is that why you brought this child? Someone dare hex, my great-granddaughter?" Obataye yelled causing Grace and Tabitha to run from the house.

"Oh, my Lord it's my heart returned to me! I missed you so much! And who is this?" Grace shouted as she ran over to hug Sadie, then looked at Cleo.

"I miss you too mama. She is your great-granddaughter, Cleo." Sadie said through her tears.

"Oh, my heart is overjoyed!" Grace said kissing Cleo on her cheeks and giving her a big hug.

"What about me? Do you miss your sister as well?" Tabitha said staring down at her sister with tears in her eyes.

"Of course!" Sadie exclaimed throwing her arms around her sister.

Seeing the twins reunited after decades brought tears to both their parent's eyes. Sadie was so caught up in joining with her family, that she almost forgot why she came.

"Papa said someone hexed Cleo?" Tabitha asked, snapping Sadie back to the reason she made the trip in the first place.

"Not me, the daughter of the people grandma works for. Cleo responded.

"The young woman I was hired to care for years ago when I left. She has crossed a powerful witch, and my power alone can't break the spell." Sadie stated.

"This White girl, what did she do to cross this witch?" Obataye asked.

"I am not sure Papa, this girl is so evil she could have done anything to any number of people, to make someone hex her." Answered Sadie.

"If she is so evil, then why help her at all?" quizzed Grace.

"Because I promised her cousin I would help her. I raised them both since they were little girls and her cousin has always loved me and treated me with respect. I am doing this for her." Replied Sadie.

Seeing the desperation in their daughter's eyes, they agreed to help. They set up the ingredients and performed the ritual that night under the light of the full moon; when the sun rose that very next day the spell would be broken.

The strength of their powers together, not only broke Sarah's spell, but it also attracted the attention of Papa Legba who came to see if he could coax Sadie into joining her family and surrendering her soul to him.

The Loa appeared before them with his slim frame, fiery red eyes, and coal black skin. He was smoking a pipe and blowing rings of smoke in the air.

"Ah, this is a long-awaited family reunion. Sadie, it is nice for you to come for your father's final days." Legba stated.

Turning to look at her parents, Sadie quizzed "Final days? What does he mean final days?"

Placing his palms on Sadie's cheeks, Obataye responded. "It is almost time for your father to go my daughter. We have lived a long and fruitful life, and now it is almost time for my transition home."

"But I thought I would have more time with you. I just reunited with my family, and now you are taking him away from me?" Sadie asked.

"It is a part of the deal, Mon Cherie. The debt must be paid. But who is this child? She is a rare find. An innocent that is pure at heart. If I can have her, I will release your family from its debt." Legba answered.

Without thinking, Cleo offered herself in place of her grandfather. "If it's me you want. I will go with you if you release my family from their debts to you."

With a look of surprise, Legba asked: "You would come with me to release your family's debt?"

"Yes! Just leave them be." Cleo shouted.

"I will not sacrifice my great-granddaughter for my debt!" Obataye shouted.

Tabitha and Sadie wrapped their arms around Cleo, then Grace and Obataye wrapped their arms around their children enclosing them. When Legba saw the strength of love from this family, he was impacted.

"You are all willing to give your lives for each other? A bond that strong, I will not break. I release you from your debt. You may die in peace. I release your soul from my claim." Legba commanded as he disappeared.

Sadie and her family hugged and rejoiced in one another for the remainder of the night. In the morning, Sadie and Cleo returned to tell Suzanne that she broke the spell, but Sadie promised to return to her family again.

Chapter Twelve

What One Witch Joins Together, Let No One Put Asunder

Neither Sarah nor anyone else in the family had heard anything from Helena, and she had not returned from her trip to visit her parents in New Orleans, but Sarah had not lost track of her. Although Helena had left North Carolina and wasn't an immediate threat, she was still quite dangerous.

Sarah knew that Helena still harbored an obsession for John and hatred for Marie. She also knew that when Helena found out they had escaped to Canada together with the twins, her rage would be uncontrollable. So just like she had done with Peter's rabid racist Uncle Thaddeus years ago, Sarah held on to Helena's gris-gris.

Although Sarah was not actively torturing Helena, she was keeping her off balance to dissuade her from focusing on John and Marie. Sarah figured the embarrassment of pretending a slave child was her own and raising him as such was enough to keep Helena from telling anyone the truth about John Jr. In case it wasn't, she wanted to keep her too preoccupied with her sanity to delve any deeper into

John and his family's whereabouts, or the secrets that drove them to Canada in the first place.

Sarah's spell had continued to keep her family safe and undiscovered until someone discovered the hex itself. Now the very thing Sarah had used to protect her family's secrets may be the very thing that brings those secrets to light.

Back in North Carolina, Sarah was as close to heaven on earth as anyone could be. Her daughter and grandchildren were safe and lived a life with more opportunity in Canada. Her son was going to make a living for himself there as well. She was reunited with the love of her life and not under the threat of slavery, and she had managed to keep Helena so off balanced that she was no longer a threat to her family…until now.

At the very instance that Sadie broke the tie between Sarah and Helena, Sarah felt it and woke from her sleep. She began breathing heavy and was sitting straight up in the bed.

"Whus wrong hummingbird?" Nathaniel asked after being startled out of his sleep.

Sarah jumped from the bed and began talking to herself while pacing about the room.

"No this can't be. Not now. Not when everyone in my family is finally happy! How? How did this happen? Who would be vile enough to help that monster and powerful enough to break my spell? What is gonna happen now? Oh lord, what's gonna happen to my baby now?" Sarah asked looking up at the ceiling.

"What ya talkin' 'bout hummingbird? Ya ain't making no sense." Nathaniel said trying to decipher what happened to make his wife so upset.

"The spell Nathaniel. The spell I put on Helena all those years ago to protect Marie and our family from that viper! Someone broke it!" Sarah said frantically.

"Who would do dat? Who would hep somebody lak Helena?" Nathaniel asked.

Sarah clutched her chest while staring out the window at the morning sun and said "I don't know Nathaniel, but whoever they are they have just painted a target on my family's back and gave Helena the bow and the arrow. When Helena realizes that she is free, nothing will keep her from hunting down Marie and her family."

Getting up to console his wife, Nathaniel said "Don't fret hummingbird, Helena ain't got no idea where dey are. Dey are gonna be fine."

Hugging her husband, Sarah replied. From your lips to God's ears. I pray you are right. All Marie's life I kept my promise to you to keep her as safe as I could. Now for the first time in her life, I am powerless to protect her. All I can do is get down on my knees and pray to the lord or bargain with the devil because only someone higher than me can help them now!"

Nathaniel broke away from his wife's embrace and started putting on his clothes. Sarah looked at her husband with a puzzled stare.

"Where are you going, Nate?" Sarah asked.

"Ta wak Pete. You don gud all des years takin care of my lil girl. Now it's my turn. I ain't 'bout ta let dat coppa head snake hurt my baby! I hang by the noose fa snapping her neck first!" Nathaniel announced, as he left to find Peter.

Nathaniel knocked so frantically at Peter's door that it scared him. Jumping out of bed, Peter rushed to open the door and saw a frantic Nathaniel standing there breathing heavily.

"Good God Nate. You almost scared me half to death. What on earth is going on that you are standing at my door at this ungodly hour?" Peter quizzed.

"Sorry Pete, but da kids are in danga. Sarah said somebody done broke da spell, and she was sho dat as soon as Helena find out, she gon head straight to find them!" Nathaniel replied.

Peter's face went white as a sheet as he thought about the danger his family was going be facing. He needed to warn them, so he decided to write them a letter. Peter knew that it was too complicated to explain everything in a letter, so he informed Marie and John that he and Marie's parents were coming to Canada for a visit. Peter had heard that Helena was in an institution, so he knew she wasn't about to just be released that quickly, so that would buy them some time. Peter told them that the visit was to celebrate the twins upcoming birthday and spend some time with them. After he pinned the letter and sent it off, he had to prepare. They were about to take that trip to see the kids that they always talked about since John and Marie moved to Canada.

Peter instructed Nathaniel to inform Sarah that they should start readying themselves. As soon as Peter could arrange it, they were going to Canada. If hell was indeed about to release that demon, he was not about to let his family face her alone.

The same feeling that woke Sarah out of her sleep in North Carolina had also snapped Helena out of her slumber. She couldn't pinpoint what was going on, but she suddenly felt different. She felt like she was her old self again, a feeling that she had not felt in years.

Helena felt the absence of the dark presence that had been such a constant companion all these years. She couldn't remember it not being there. Finally, after all this time, she was free; and now that her mind was open, she could work on freeing her body from this prison. Helena fell back asleep, but now the feeling of fear and dread that were her usual bedfellows were replaced with peace and hope.

That night marked the turning point in Helena's "recovery" and at her cousin Suzanne's next visit, she informed Helena of what had caused her past mental state. Suzanne also revealed that she had enlisted the help of another powerful voodoo priestess to remove it, but she kept Sadie's identity a secret as she had promised.

Armed with this information, Helena began to feel empowered. She started making her exit strategy by playing on Dr. Bastian's narcissistic belief that he could cure her "psychosis." She complimented him, and she played the role of the excellent and compliant patient flawlessly.

Dr. Bastian was so caught up in praising himself that he couldn't see that Helena was playing him. Soon Helena had convinced him that his treatments had indeed cured her and that she was well enough to return home. Less than three months after Sadie broke Sarah's spell, Helena was preparing to re-enter her old life. She completed her last session with Dr. Bastian, politely nodding and agreeing with every idiotic thing he was saying while thinking of what she was going to do first once she was finally on the other side of those gates.

When the session was over, Helena returned to her room and grabbed her things and went to the waiting area. Looking around at what had been her home for the last nine years and what she thought would be her tomb, Helena wept. She was overjoyed to be leaving this place behind her, and she promised herself that she would not waste another day of her precious life thinking about it.

Helena's mulling was interrupted by the familiar sound of her parents. She turned to see them standing at the end of the hall, and she ran to embrace them. The feeling of having their little girl back was so overwhelming that they didn't want ever to let her go.

After signing all her exit paperwork, Helena gathered her things and walked out those enormous double doors for the last time. She didn't even turn around to give them a farewell glance. From that point on, Helena promised herself she was going to put that place and everything that led up to her being there in the past and focus on the future.

On the ride home, Helena felt as if she was in a strange new world. A lot had changed during the time she had been away, and she planned to discover every bit of it. As they pulled up to the Marchand plantation, emotion overcame Helena. She thought she would never see this place again and now she was home.

When the carriage came to a stop, Helena did not wait for the driver to escort her out. She bounded from the transport and ascended the steps two at a time. She had just been released from hell, so she felt she could forego formalities, at least for a little while.

Bursting into the house, Helena went from place to place soaking up every inch of it. When she finally reached her room, she ran in and dived on the bed. The soft feather bed felt like a hug from an old friend. She lay on her back looking around her room. Helena felt her yellow walls were like being surrounded by the sun, and she intended to bask in its glow.

Staring at all her familiar surroundings, Helena was immensely grateful that her parents had chosen to keep her room just as she left it. All she wanted to do was lay on her bed and rest. Once her strength returned, she would think about what to do with the rest of her life; but for now, she was just grateful that decision is now hers to make.

Back to Normal

After a few weeks of getting adjusted to her surroundings again, Helena was now able to think clearly; and one of the things she was thinking about was John and John Jr. She had been away so long and under such mental anguish that she had little time to wonder where they were and why they had not come looking for her.

"Are you up Miss?" Cleo asked after knocking on Helena's door.

"Yes. You may come in." Helena said. She had been up for an hour already, and she was dressed and sitting at her vanity.

Cleo opened the door and entered Helena's room carrying a tray of food. When Helena saw Cleo, she looked puzzled.

"I don't believe I have ever seen you before. Who are you? Where is Sadie?" Helena asked?

Sitting the tray down on a table beside Helena's bed, Cleo answered. "My name Cleo Miss. I'm Sadie's granddaughter. She old and sick, so I look afta you now. Miz Marchand tole me ta brang breakfast up to you."

Helena looked intensely at Cleo, studying her every feature. She was beautiful. Her face was soft and innocent, but her eyes indicated there was more there than meets the eye. Her complexion, hair, and figure coupled with her striking beauty reminded Helena of a young Marie, which pleased Helena very much.

It was as if she could have Marie waiting on her every need all over again. It also reignited the jealousy and rage that she harbored for Marie since they were teenagers. Once Helena left the hospital, she began to obsess over Marie and John and to see Cleo just furthered those obsessive thoughts.

Cleo noticed the intensely strange stares that Helena was giving her, and they were starting to make her very uncomfortable.

"You alright Miss?" Cleo asked, snapping Helena out of her Nostalgia.

Shaking her head in an attempt snap back to reality, Helena answered. "Yes, yes of course I am. Was there something else Cleo?"

"Yes, miss. Miz. Marchand wont me to tell you dat dere wuz a guest waitin in da Parla ta visit wit ya. Ya cuzin Suzanne." Cleo stated.

"Please tell her to come up Cleo, and I would like us not to be disturbed. Helena instructed.

"Yes, miss," Cleo replied and exited the room.
In her obsession, Helena had asked her cousin to discretely inquire about what was going on with John and her son. In the spirit of full disclosure, Helena had told Suzanne everything about her arranged marriage to John and the twins actual

paternity. Secrets which Suzanne swore to take to her grave. Helena knew that Suzanne was coming today to give her a full report on what was going on, so she had been eagerly awaiting her arrival.

When Suzanne walked in, Helena was standing at the window.

"Hello cousin. How are you feeling?" Suzanne asked kissing Helena on both cheeks.

"Anxious. What did you find out about my family?" Helena inquired.

Holding Helena's hands, Suzanne led her over to the bed to sit.

"Well, it wasn't easy, but I found out that John and John Jr. are no longer in North Carolina," Suzanne stated.

Helena's heart sank, and she moved in closer as if she was trying to read the answers in Suzanne's face.

"What do you mean? Where are they?" Helena asked.

"Well, from what I have gathered from my sources in North Carolina, John, John Jr., Marie and her son TJ fled to Canada. They are living in Chatham, Canada and John is an assistant for a local abolitionist there named John Scoble." Suzanne said.

"So, while I am locked away in a loony bin, my dear husband flees the country to live with his mistress and their bastard children?" Helen shouted

"That slave bitch has been the source of my unhappiness for far too long. It is because of her that John could not bring himself to love me. I bet she put some spell on him. I bet she is the one who put a spell on me!" quipped Helena now pacing the room.

"Well, if she thinks that she can run off with my husband to Canada and have a fairytale ending she is sadly mistaken. I have lived in hell in that asylum for the last nine years, and now that I know it is because of her, I will not rest until I turn her dreams into a nightmare!" Helena scoffed.

Helena's demeanor made Suzanne question if she was mad. The sheer glee she saw in Helena's eyes at the thought of inflicting sorrow on Marie and John was that of a person who was not well.

"Helena, there is more. While you were in the asylum, John was able to get a divorce. He is no longer your husband, so you must let this go, darling, you just got home. Enjoy your life and forget about John and Marie. You have no proof that it was Marie who cast the spell; you have no shortage of servants and former slaves that may wish ill-will on you. And if it was Marie or someone close to her, who did this to you, you should not tempt fate or their wrath again." Suzanne pleaded.

Turning around with an eerily calm look in her eyes, Helena responded. "Oh, dear cousin. It is they that should fear my wrath. I will leave for Canada by week's end. Tell Cleo to pack my bags and ready herself. She is going to accompany me on my little trip. There are some old friends that I simply must visit."

Helena was moving about the room in a frenzy; then she suddenly stopped in the middle of the floor as if someone had flipped off a switch.

"What day is it?" Helena quizzed.

Looking confused as to why Helena was suddenly so concerned with the date, Suzanne responded. "It is the first of October. Why do you ask?"

A sinister smile came over Helena's face, and she began laughing hysterically. The action was so startling to Suzanne; she jumped back almost falling. Suzanne braced herself against the wall as she watched Helena dart about the room in a somewhat manic state.

"My dear sweet cousin, it is almost my fake son's 18th birthday! The timing is perfect! I will tell daddy that I think it is time to bring John Jr. back to New Orleans so that he can start to learn the family business. As much as my father professes to love me, I know that love increased when I gave him a male heir. Now I can bring his heir home with me to New Orleans. It will endear my father to me and rip Marie's heart right out of her chest!"

Realizing that her attempts to reason with Helena had fallen on deaf ears, she shook her head with tears in her eyes. Who had her cousin become? Had all that time in the asylum indeed driven her mad? Or was she insane before she even went in? Suzanne left to find Cleo and deliver the message as well as arrange for her cousin's travel to Canada.

As much as she loved her cousin, Suzanne knew that this would be the last time that she saw her. She could no longer try to save the woman who she once thought of like a sister, that woman never came home from East Louisiana Hospital. In fact, Suzanne was beginning to believe that woman had died the day she let her obsession with John take over her life.

Helena was so focused on her plan that she didn't even notice when Suzanne left. Helena went to her father and told him of her intentions; and although he wasn't happy about her traveling so far after just getting home, he agreed. Alexander gave her the address of his old friends the Dumas, who had moved there.

Alexander told Helena that the friend would provide room and board for the duration of her stay, and he would send them a letter about her impending arrival. By the end of the week, Helena and Cleo headed to Canada and John, and Marie was about to get a very unexpected and unwelcomed visitor.

Chapter Fourteen

New Wife, New Life

When John arrived in Canada with his family in 1865, he immediately went to the address of the safe house the old minister had given him. It belonged to an older White couple who gave John and his family room and board until they could get set up in a home of their own.

The woman was an advocate for human rights and had been a part of the underground railroad. The man was an abolitionist who was friends with John Scoble, the man for whom John was going to be working as an assistant.

John Scoble was a proponent for the rights of Blacks. He had worked with the British and Foreign anti-slavery society and worked to free slaves in France. However, he did not have good relations with some of those in the United States who fought for the end of slavery, including anti-slavery advocate William Lloyd Garrison and his supporters.

Scoble came to Canada in 1852 to lend his assistance to the British American Institute of Science and Industry, a vocational school for fugitive slaves. A fugitive slave turned abolitionist,

Minister Josiah Henson initially started it after he, his wife and four children escaped slavery and fled to Canada. Henson had started the school as part of the Dawn Township; a self-sufficient community developed in Kent County, to give slaves that escaped to Canada a fresh start.

The township, initially set on 200 acres of land, became very prosperous reaching numbers of around 500 people at its height; and exporting black walnut lumber to both the United States and Britain. Henson eventually purchased an additional 200 acres beside the settlement where he lived with his family.

Henson and Scoble had disputes that impeded Scoble's efforts to restructure the institute's finances, which made the entire reason Scoble came to Canada in the first place, a source of contention. Although he wasn't making headway with his original plan for coming to Canada, he felt he could still be of influence.

Despite facing opposition from his efforts at the school, Scoble continued to advocate for the rights of escaped slaves. In 1860, he stopped a fugitive slave accused of murder, named John Anderson from being deported back to Missouri. However, in 1861, Scoble's disputes with Henson as well as the Board of Trustees, caused him to resign from the Institute's Board. The school later closed in 1868, and its property sold. An integrated school in Chatham received the monies from the sell.

In 1863, Scoble won an election for the Legislative Assembly of the Providence of Canada. He replaced the original selected official, George

Macbeth, who was removed after his election to the office was declared invalid. Later that year, Scoble was then reelected in the general election.

John felt honored to be working for such a great man and excited to learn as much from him as possible, but he still didn't feel comfortable enough to let his new boss or anyone else know that he was Black or any of his other family secrets.

If John were honest, he and Marie would probably have moved into a little cabin in Dawn's Township in Kent County. That is where most of the other Blacks lived when they fled to Canada, but because he was still passing as White, they settled in a little house in the neighboring county of Chatham.

John and Marie had not even told the boys that they were twins; or that he and Marie were their biological parents. Marie had grappled with the decision to continue to hide this secret every day. It ripped her apart that even with Helena out of the way, she was still on the outside looking in when it came to one of her sons.

John and Marie were finally in a place where they could be happy as a family, yet they were not wholly living as one. The lies they told to protect their family in North Carolina, was keeping them from being a family in Canada.

Every day that Marie looked at her sons, she wanted to tell them that their mother loves them. They were in a place where no one knew them, and they could be free to love each other as they were. It was what she had always dreamed of, but now that her dream was here, it was still just outside of her reach.

How could she tell her sons that she was their mother? One always knew she was and the other never conceived she could be. A forbidden love created their very existence, and their lives were predicated on a web of deceit that was once readily cast and was now impossible to untangle.

Through the years, the boys had lots of questions about why they had to move to Canada in the first place; and why Helena never came back. John and Marie had done their best to try to avoid answering those questions for now, but they knew it was only a matter of time before they could no longer be silent.

Marie tried to immerse herself in Canadian life. She learned everything she could from the older woman with whom they were staying, about the Canadian society; and what was accepted and expected. The woman was kind and motherly, which made it a little easier for Marie being so far away from her mother.

Once John and Marie had gotten settled into their new home, Marie focused on her family. She made sure she got the boys enrolled in school, got their house set up, kept her family fed and in clean clothes. Once she got everyone else settled into their lives, she started thinking about her own.

There weren't a lot of opportunities or choices for Blacks in the United States, especially women, so Marie had never given what she wanted for her life much thought. Now that they were in this strange new land with more possibilities, Marie wondered what may be possible for her.

Marie had liked writing stories ever since she first learned to read and write on the Devereux plantation. She would write beautiful stories about faraway lands where slavery didn't exist, and everyone was equal, but she never shared them with anyone.

When Marie learned about a Black woman author named Harriet E. Wilson, who wrote her autobiography in 1859 entitled *Sketches from the Life of a Free Black*, she was intrigued. She wondered if there were more books written by Blacks.

Marie's search turned up a book written in 1852 by another Black woman author named Harriet Beecher Stowe, entitled *Uncle Tom's Cabin*. It further fueled her interest when she learned that not only was that book based on the life of an actual person named Josiah Henson, but he was an author as well.

Josiah Henson had also written his autobiography in 1849 entitled, *The Life of Josiah Henson, formerly a slave, now an inhabitant of Canada.* Reading the title alone gave her hope. The man who wrote his story from slavery to freedom was right there in Canada. Immediately Marie knew somehow she had to meet him.

Knowing that these people had taken their destiny into their own hands and wrote their own story, gave Marie courage. She started thinking about writing her novel someday. Marie had no idea how to write a professional book; she was just happy that for the first time in her life, it was a possibility.

Marie began to ask around about Josiah. She learned that he was an abolitionist and methodist preacher; and that he spoke on routes between Tennessee and Ontario. The next time he spoke, she made sure she was in the crowd to see him, introducing herself and telling him about how much he inspired her.

Josiah invited her to come to his home and meet his family, and Marie happily accepted his invitation. She met his wife Nancy and their four children. Marie listened to his experiences and life's journey from his lips. She enjoyed her time with the Henson family very much, and this would be one of many trips she would make to Dawn's Township.

Her new friendship with the Henson family was only one of the many things Marie loved about Canada. She enjoyed her new home and all its newfound freedoms, but once the excitement of moving into their own home and getting settled into Canadian life had started to die down, she became homesick. So, when her brother Jacob arrived on their doorstep, Marie's heart burst open with joy.

Jacob stayed with John and Marie for a few months to get acclimated to his new surroundings and catch up with his family. He marveled at how much the twins had grown and how happy they seemed to be in their new home.

Jacob also gave them an update on Helena. When he told them that Helena was in an insane asylum, John immediately started the paperwork to expedite their divorce, so he could to marry Marie.

Jacob also filled them in on what happened when he returned to North Carolina; and how he almost became a dead war hero. Both John and Marie were familiar with the McAllisters and all the unfortunate souls that met their end because of them. Marie knew that Jacob's life would have been in constant danger in North Carolina, so she was so grateful that Peter was able to get him safe passage to Canada. Having her brother there with her helped to ease her feelings of being homesick just a bit, but she still longed to see her parents.

Marie introduced Jacob to the Henson family, and Josiah helped Jacob get a job exporting black walnut lumber. Jacob purchased a little cabin in Dawn's Township, and then he quickly made the acquaintance of a beautiful young woman named Annie. She worked as a maid for the Dumas family in neighboring Chatham. Meeting Annie helped Jacob's transition to Canadian life even better than he ever expected.

Marie's surprise of having her brother so close made her both happy and sad. She was delighted that she had another family member there with her but sorry that the rest of her family could not enjoy this new life with her as well. Now that Jacob was also in Dawn's township, Marie had even more reason to visit.

John wrote his family in North Carolina and let them know that Jacob had arrived safely and that he was set up with lodging and a job. He also told them of his plan to divorce Helena and marry Marie. An event he hoped they would be able to attend when it finally arrived.

The arrival of Jacob and John's pending divorce from Helena was the best news their family had received in a long time. The boys were beginning to grow closer as brothers, and everyone was bonding together as a family. John Jr. was even open to his father moving on with his life, given that his mother had been committed to the insane asylum.

Strangely, Marie had always felt like more of a mother to John Jr. than Helena did anyway, but he never admitted that to anyone. He knew that Helena was supposed to be his mother, but he never felt connected to her. His father marrying Marie would just solidify the family they had already started to build.

It finally appeared to be peace and happiness among the Jean Baptiste Monets and the Devereux families. Little did anyone know it was just the quiet before the storm.

Chapter Fifteen

Same Helena, Different Country

Fall 1874

It was a crisp October morning, and Marie awoke with a feeling of peace and joy that had become common. She and her family had been in Canada for ten years now, John was granted a divorce from Helena and married her, and the twins were about to celebrate their 18th birthday.

Marie's heart was overflowing with happiness. They had not heard anything from or about Helena since she had been committed, and Marie and John had renewed their love for each other. Now, her family was coming to visit.

Since Helena had left before John and Marie moved with the boys to Canada, John told John Jr. that his mother decided she didn't want to be a wife and mother anymore, so she went back to New Orleans to start her life over there.

When they discovered that Helena was in an insane asylum with no indication of ever being released, John Jr. willing accepted Marie assuming the role of the mother in his life. Unbeknownst to John Jr, that role was rightfully Marie's.

Marie had been running around getting everything prepared for the twins' 18th birthday, and her family's visit. Peter was arriving that day along with Sarah and Nathaniel. Jacob and his wife Annie were even coming over to help her prepare for the festivities.

For the first time in a decade, Marie was going to have her entire family under one roof. She was so overjoyed. Marie thought nothing could spoil her happiness. She had no idea that one guest was arriving that wasn't on the list. This guest was not coming to share in Marie's happiness, this guest was coming to destroy it.

Helena and Cleo arrived in Canada and took refuge at her father's friends' house. After she and Cleo got settled into their quarters, Helena decided to pump her hosts for information. She figured that was the best place to start inquiring about how to find her family. Helena came down for dinner, and Cleo ate with the servants. Helena had instructed her to find out what she could from them as well.

"Please come and join us, sweetheart. I know you must be ravenous after such a long journey." Mrs. Dumas beckoned.

Politely nodding and sitting down at the table, Helena joined her hosts for dinner.

"So, tell us, dear, what brings you to Canada?" Mr. Dumas inquired.

"Oh, I just wanted to get away for a little while and figured I would just come for a visit." Helena lied.

"Well, it's lovely to see you again dear. We had not laid eyes on you since you were a small child. Tomorrow I will take you into town to look around and maybe do some shopping Mrs. Dumas stated.

"That sounds wonderful Mrs. Dumas," Helena replied with a fake smile.

Helena was looking forward to her trip to town, but it wasn't to go shopping. She had planned to locate the office of Mr. Scoble. She figured if she could identify where John worked she could then find out where he and Marie lived. The thought was making a sinister smile come over her face.

Helena excused herself, after sitting through an hour of mindless chit-chat. She stated she was tired from the long journey, then headed straight for Cleo's room to see if she turned up anything. Cleo informed her that she had not, but that she had asked one of the servants if she could tag along when she went to the market the next morning.

Helena was pleased. She informed Cleo they would meet up again the next night to share what they each had learned. That night, Helena slept peacefully and dreamed of exacting revenge on John and Marie.

The next morning Helena awoke early, anxious to get started with her search for John and Marie. Cleo had already left to accompany the Dumas' servant Annie to the market.

"So, what brings you to Canada?" Annie asked.

"Miss Helena's father didn't wont her to travel all dis way by herself, so I came wit her," Cleo said.

"So, what's it like in America?" Annie asked. Looking around at how freely Blacks moved about in Canada interacting with Whites, Cleo answered "Nuthin like dis."

"What do you mean?" Annie asked.

Cleo stopped to look around again, then pointed at a White man and Black man shaking hands and being cordial.

"Lik dose men ova dare, shakin hans like dey friends. You don't see dat back home. Where I'm from if a White man is touchin a Black man it's to put a noose 'round his neck." Cleo said.

Annie stood there looking into Cleo's eyes for a minute without speaking. She had heard stories about America, and she knew a lot of slaves had escaped to Canada but being born in Canada Annie had never experienced first-hand the horrors that Cleo was describing. Annie was in school and only working at the Dumas' house until graduation. She couldn't imagine someone telling her that she could not leave or beat her for some perceived infraction.

"I am so sorry that you came from such a horrible place Cleo, but if it is so bad in America, why go back? You know you don't have to. You could stay here and get a job, go to school, or do whatever you want to do." Annie suggested.

Cleo stood there for a minute letting that thought sink into her head. *Could she stay here? What did Cleo have left? The only person she had was her grandma, and she had gone to the Bayou to spend her last days with her parents and sister* before Cleo left for Canada. Cleo knew that her grandma wanted her to have the best life possible, and she was not going to be able to do that in America.

Cleo didn't answer Annie, but she was thinking about it. She was in such deep thought that she wasn't paying attention to where she was going and almost walked right in front of a carriage. Right before she stepped off the curb, Cleo felt a pair of strong hands snatch her back just in time.

"Oh, my goodness TJ thank you so much! I wasn't even paying attention. She would have surely been hit had you not pulled her back. "Annie exclaimed.

A startled Cleo pushed away from her rescuer to regain her footing.

"Is dat what Y'all do heh? Grab women on da street?!?" Cleo said agitated that she was thrown to the ground.

"When they blindly step off the curb into the path of a carriage we do. It's called saving your life, and you're welcome." TJ said.

"Oh, so I 'posed to thank you, fa jerkin me round like a ragdoll?" Cleo asked dusting her dress off and still getting her bearings.

"Better to be jerked like a rag doll, then ground into the dust by a carriage." TJ retorted.

A defiant Cleo was about to return TJ's sarcasm until she looked up and saw his gorgeous face. At that moment her words got lost in her throat. She saw his lips moving so she knew he was talking, but her mind couldn't process the words. She was in shock from the near-death experience and awe of the handsome stranger who saved her.

"I said are you ok?" TJ asked noticing Cleo had suddenly lost her ability to speak.

Cleo regained her composure then responded "Yes. Sorry, fa pushin you. I guess I shoulda been lookin where I was goin'."

When Cleo calmed down and stopped slinging insults at TJ, he noticed just how beautiful she was. Seeing the apparent connection brewing between her new friend and her nephew, Annie interjected "This is my nephew TJ. TJ this is my new friend Cleo. She is visiting from America. New Orleans I think."

"New Orleans huh? I was born there." TJ said.

"Really? I ain't neva seen you befo" Cleo said.

"Well, I didn't grow up there. My family moved to North Carolina when I was just an infant, so I have no real memory of the place. But now that I have met you, I think my birthplace must be a pretty special place." TJ stated.

"Why you say dat? Cleo asked looking confused.

"Because if one as beautiful and feisty as you reside there, it can't help but be special," TJ said still looking into Cleo's eyes.

Cleo started to blush and smile. She was intrigued by TJ. She had never met anyone like him before.

"You talk funny, but I like it," Cleo said blushing.

"Well, I hope that I get the opportunity to talk to you again while you are here. Make amends for the way we met." TJ responded.

"I thank I wud like dat" Cleo replied.

"Good. Then meet me here in the square tomorrow at noon. I would love to show you around." TJ offered.

"OK" was all Cleo could manage to speak at that point. Her voice was competing with the sound of her heart thumping fiercely in her chest and the feeling of butterflies in her stomach."

"I will see you tomorrow. Try to stay on the curb until then ok?" TJ said with a smirk.

Trying not to smile, Cleo playfully pushed TJ's shoulder and replied: "You try not to throw nobody on tha groun til den."

The two held each other's gaze, and they parted ways. After meeting TJ, Cleo forgot all about trying to pry information out of Annie about the family Helena planned to destroy. Now the only information she wanted to know was everything about TJ and his family. Little did she know they were one and the same.

Chapter Sixteen

I Once Was Lost, But Now I'm Found

That evening, TJ filled his family in on the beautiful visitor that he had encountered earlier, and Annie informed them that Cleo was accompanying a house guest of the family she worked for and that they were from New Orleans. Peter, Sarah, and Nathaniel both looked like they had seen a ghost. They had gotten so caught up in enjoying seeing their children and grandchildren and hearing about their new life; they didn't want to ruin it just yet with talk of Helena. However, when Annie said the guests were from New Orleans, they were all wondering if it was Helena.

"Annie, what did you say the name of the house guest was with whom your new friend was traveling? Peter quizzed.

"I'm not sure. I have not had any interaction with my friend's traveling companion. I can find out for you when I go back to work if you like." Annie responded.

"Yes, I would thank you, dear," Peter replied.

"Is something wrong father?" John asked.

"Oh no son, I just wanted to see if it was anyone I knew, that's all," Peter responded.

Peter wasn't even sure Helena left the hospital, so he didn't want to ruin their visit unnecessarily. He decided to put off telling them just yet. Instead, he helped John make room to accommodate everyone, including Jacob and Annie, who also spent the night.

John and Marie's home was a nice size, but it wasn't anywhere close to the vast estate on which they grew up. Somehow, they felt more blessed and prosperous than they had ever felt back on Tobacco Road.

With all the people they loved gathered together in that space, their modest home was grander than the most exquisite palatial estate. This feeling of complete happiness was a feeling Peter wanted to preserve as long as possible. The twins' birthday was only a few days away, and he decided to wait until that passed. He wanted this to be a perfect celebration.

The next morning, Cleo awoke early and left before Helena had gotten out of bed. She told Mrs. Dumas to tell Helena that she had gone into town with Annie and that she would be back later that evening. Annie led Cleo back to the town square to meet up with TJ. After greeting her nephew, she told Cleo that she had some errands to run and that she would meet her back there at precisely 3:00 pm to take her back. Cleo agreed, and Annie bid her goodbye.

"Well, I'm heh. Now whut?" Cleo asked.

"Are you always this impatient?" TJ asked with a laugh.

"I'm a very busy young woman," Cleo said with a smirk.

"Well, I certainly don't want to waste your precious time young lady, so why don't we get this day started," TJ said while giving a mock bow.

Cleo returned the gesture with a mock curtsy. She couldn't keep from smiling at him, and since their meeting, she couldn't seem to get him out of her mind.

TJ led Cleo through the town, all the while giving her a tour of the city he had come to love. When they reached a small boat, TJ climbed in first and steadied it with one foot in the boat and the other on the shore. He took Cleo by the hand and helped her into the seat. She loved how she felt with TJ. He made Annie's offer of staying in Canada sound more and more appealing.

"Where we goin'? Cleo asked looking out at the water.

"I have something extraordinary I want to show you," TJ responded.

"Whut is it? Cleo quizzed.

"It's a surprise. Now stop asking so many questions and enjoy the ride." TJ quipped flashing that winning smile that made Cleo smile despite herself.

Cleo sat back and mockingly pretended to seal her lips together using an imaginary lock, then gestured throwing the imaginary key into the water. Soon she saw the most breathtaking sight that she had seen. Miles and Miles of structures of varying sizes jutting up from the surface. Some so small they could support only one tree and others large enough to accommodate castle-like houses.

"Whut is dis place? Cleo asked with eyes filled with wonder.

"They are called the thousand islands" TJ replied.

"Why dey call it dat?" Cleo quizzed.

"Because it's made up of over 1800 little islands that stretch about 50 miles and borders America and Canada. Some of the islands are in America, while others are part of Canada. They are all different sizes. Shrubs and small trees only inhabit some of the smaller ones. Others like the ones we are passing now have become prime spots for the wealthy to build their summer homes." TJ informed.

"It's so much prettier here than in America," Cleo said soaking up her surroundings.

"It's nothing compared to the beauty I see," TJ responded.

"Where?" Cleo asked looking to see what it was that she was missing.

"Here" TJ responded gently turning her face so that their eyes met, then softly kissing her lips.

Cleo felt a tingling sensation going through her body. She had just had her first kiss, and it was more magical and incredible than she ever thought possible.

Cleo was sitting on the water in a boat with a man that was as gentle as he was handsome; looking at a beauty that she never knew existed. Before this trip, she didn't know anything about Canada; now she can't imagine being anywhere else. Cleo decided at that moment, if she could find a way to stay, Helena would be returning to New Orleans alone.

Cleo wasn't the only one feeling like she should stay in Canada. TJ was in awe of this beautiful woman who was so fierce and self-assured on the surface, but vulnerable and filled with childlike wonder inside.

TJ was growing fond of the woman who was a walking contradiction, and the more time he spent with her, the more time he wanted with her. Her strength and courage made him admire her, and her childlike innocence made him want to protect her.
Time passed quickly as Cleo and TJ talked about their lives, and their likes and dislikes. Hours passed like minutes, and soon they noticed that it was past the time Cleo was supposed to meet Annie to return to the Dumas' home.

Cleo had no idea what she was going to tell Helena because she had not inquired at all about John Devereux. When they spoke of family, TJ had only talked in detail about his Black war hero father Thomas; and since Helena gave her little to no details about anyone else besides John and John Jr., she didn't connect the dots.

Cleo had no idea her budding romance with the handsome stranger could help Helena destroy the very people he loved. Although neither wanted to leave, they knew they must say goodbye, but not before they agreed to meet the next day again. When they finally arrived back to meet Annie, she was frantic. She had no idea what could have happened to Cleo, and she knew she could not return without her.

Once Annie saw that she was ok, her anxiety immediately subsided. Cleo and TJ both apologized for being late, then TJ bid them both farewell.

As the two young women walked back to the Dumas' house, Cleo filled Annie in on all the details of her date with TJ. Annie was excited about her new friend and her nephew, so she agreed to help Cleo continue to meet up with TJ.

When Cleo arrived at the house, Helena was waiting for her. "Well now, what kept you so long?" Helena asked with eyes piercing.

"Sorry miss. I loss trak uh time." Cleo answered.

"Well, it must have been something pretty important for you to be gone so long in a country you know nothing about." Helena retorted.

"I got loss Miss. Like you say I don't know nuthin bout dis place." Cleo said avoiding eye contact with Helena.

"Well, I guess you better learn to be more careful, we wouldn't want your careless mistakes to cause you undue harm, now would we?" Helena asked with an unflinching stare.

"No miss," Cleo responded with eyes cast down.

"Ok now go on to bed we have much work to do. I managed to get the location of where John works from Mr. Dumas, so now I must figure out where he lives." Helena stated.

"Yes, miss," Cleo replied and walked up the stairs to bed.

Cleo remained respectful and humble as her grandmother had taught her, to protect her family secret. Her grandmother had spent years grooming Cleo to be a mambo someday, and Cleo was a quick study. She had a natural gift. Her grandmother was the reason Helena was able to leave the asylum, but if she crossed Cleo, she was more than prepared to help her find her way back.

Chapter Seventeen

There is a Thin Line Between Love and Hate

The next morning, Cleo left with Annie to meet TJ for another date. She could hardly sleep the night before thinking about what an incredible adventure he had in store for her the next day. Although Cleo tried her best to hide her rendezvous from Helena, her sudden elation had made Helena more than a little suspicious. Helena had the feeling that Cleo was losing her focus on why she was supposed to be in Canada in the first place, but she would have to deal with her later. She had more pressing matters to attend.

Helena had got dressed early that morning and went to stake out John's place of employment. She stood across the street for a while trying to get her plan together, when the door opened. Helena's heart stopped beating for a moment as she saw John walking out of the office. He was heading down the block to grab lunch at his favorite pub. Seeing him again flooded Helena with emotions she thought she had overcome. She had let her hatred for John and Marie fester for so long that she thought those were the only feelings she had left, she was wrong.

Seeing John again made Helena feel like she was drowning in a sea of conflicting emotions. She hated that he divorced her while she was in the asylum and married her mortal enemy, but seeing him also rekindled the feeling of love that Helena thought she buried long ago.

When Helena finally snapped out of her trance, and she was sure that John had entered the pub, she hurried across the street to see if she could probe his boss for information. Helena straightened her dress and smoothed her hair from her face. She regained her composure, so she could focus on the task at hand, then walked into the office. An older White gentleman looked up from his desk and asked "Can I help you, miss?

With a big smile and deliberate tone, Helena responded: "Well I certainly hope so. Does John Devereux work here?"

"Yes, he does, do you have an appointment with him?" the man asked.

"Not exactly, see I am an old friend of his from New Orleans. We grew up together on neighboring plantations, and I heard he had moved to Canada. So naturally, when I came to visit some dear family friends, the Dumas, I thought it would be great to catch up."

"Oh, that's nice, I am sure he will be happy to see you. If you are from the states, you must know his lovely wife Marie and their beautiful children." The old man said.

Hearing the man refer to Marie as John's wife and the twins as "their" children, was enough to send

Helena over the edge. It was almost impossible for Helena to hide her anger, but she clenched her teeth and replied. "Oh goodness yes, we are all old friends who used to play together."

The man noticed the change in her demeanor and began to question her. "John will be back in a few minutes; would you like to wait for him?"

Helena did not want to let John know she was in Canada until she could carry out her plan, so she responded, "Well I would love to, but I have some business I have to attend to, so if you could just give me his home address, I will just surprise him and his lovely wife at home."

The man got an eerie feeling that Helena was not being completely honest about why she was looking for John, so he said. "I'm sorry miss, but I cannot give you that information, but as I said if you would like to wait, he should be back in a minute."

Helena did not want to run the risk of John coming back and finding her there, so she quickly tried to make her exit. "You know what, I will just come back and try to catch him later, but I really must be going."

"What did you say your name was again miss? I will tell him you stopped by." The man quizzed.

"Oh, that really won't be necessary, I want to surprise him, so I will just come back another time. Thank you and nice meeting you." Helena said as she hurried out the door, narrowly missing John who was walking back to the office.

When he entered the office, the old man informed John about his strange visitor.

"There was a woman here to see you a few minutes ago, in fact, you may have passed her on your way in, she just left." The old man stated.

"A visitor? From where? What was her name?" John quizzed.

"Don't know her name, she didn't want to tell me. She said you grew up together in New Orleans, and she knew you and your wife. She is staying with some old family friends in town by the name of Dumas. She was acting very strange and wanted your home address to surprise you. I asked her if she wanted to wait until you returned to the office, but she declined and left in a hurry." The man replied.

John found it very odd and asked the man to describe the visitor. His description could be a dead ringer for Helena, but John knew that Helena was locked up in the Asylum in New Orleans, and even if she was out, she had no idea where they were so that couldn't be her. Still, the description sent chills down his spine.

John decided to push the thought of Helena finding him and his family out of his head for now, but he was going ask his family for an update on her possible release date when he arrived home. John threw himself back into his work day as best he could, but he still could not shake the sinking feeling in the pit of his stomach.

Across the street, Helena was having the equivalent of a mini break down. "I was so close to finding their little love nest! The nerve of that old man to ask me if I knew John's lovely wife! I AM HIS LOVELY WIFE!!!!" Helena screamed.

Helena was so caught up in her emotions that she didn't realize that her tantrum was starting to draw attention. When she came to her senses, and regained her composure, she started to head back to the Dumas' house. Feeling dejected, Helena thought her efforts today were a total loss, that is until she saw just what her traveling companion had been up to all this time. Cleo was across the street, apparently enamored by a handsome young man with whom she was having a conversation. Upon closer inspection, she saw that young man was none other than Thomas Childress, Jr. Helena could not help but laugh at the thought that Cleo's new love was going to lead her to her old one.

I Spy, Someone I Want to Die

Cleo and TJ were meeting for another beautiful afternoon together. This time, he wanted to take her to hear famed abolitionist Frederick Douglas speak at an event in the town square. Helena decided that she would follow Cleo to see if she could lead her to where John and Marie lived.

"How is that you get more beautiful each time I see you?" TJ asked as he kissed Chloe on her cheek.

Cleo giggled and looked down at the ground trying to hide that she was blushing and replied "I'ont know. This is just how I look."

TJ chuckled at how cute Cleo was when she was embarrassed, then took her hand to lead her to their destination.

"So, where you say we goin' again?" Cleo asked.

"To see a great abolitionist named Frederick Douglas speak. TJ replied.

Looking confused, Cleo asked "What's a abolishnis?

Captivated by her childlike thirst for learning, TJ repeated "Ab-o-li-tion-ist."

"dats wut I sed. Now wut is it? Cleo asked again.

"An abolitionist is someone who opposes slavery. They were instrumental in ending slavery." TJ responded.

"So, if slavery awredy ended, don' dat mean he out of a job? So wut he got ta talk 'bout nah? Cleo quizzed.

"As you well know, just because they legally ended the institution of slavery, it doesn't mean our people are free. Coming from New Orleans, I am sure you know that the fight for equality is not over. More Blacks are dying now than when they were slaves." TJ stated.

Cleo loved being around TJ, he knew so much about so many things, he was much more educated than the boys Cleo knew. It made Cleo want to know more as well. When they arrived at the square, they found a spot to watch the speech. There was already a significant crowd gathered, so TJ was glad they were able to find a place close to the stage. Helena remained in the shadows, but close enough not to lose sight of the couple.

"Ugh, I can't believe I have to sit here and listen to this self-righteous negro speak! If this is this boy's idea of a date, he has a lot to learn about women! Cleo better not get any ideas from listening to this foolishness." Helena said trying to get closer to hear what they were saying to each other.

Cleo had never heard Frederick Douglas speak before, nor even knew who he was. When he came onto the stage, Cleo instantly felt that she was in the presence of someone great. As he began to speak, Cleo became entranced. She had never heard a negro talk so eloquently, and it made Cleo want to learn to improve her speech as well. Cleo took in every word like a starving man consumes food. She was receiving food for thought that was slowly feeding her soul. There at a speech about the true meaning of freedom, Cleo started thinking more about her own. Canada had shown Cleo so many great things, more than America ever hoped to, and she had no intention of letting them go. Now she just had to figure out how to free herself from Helena.

When the speech was over, TJ escorted Cleo back to meet Annie. As they were walking, he was interested in her thoughts about what she had heard, and she was eager to share them.

"So, what did you think?" TJ quizzed.

"I ain't neva herd nutthin like that befo. He talked 'bout eva'body be'in equal; and how much Blacks hav don fo dis country. How we had ta edjacate ourself and free our mines. It makes me want ta do betta. I wonta go ta school lak you. Maybe stay heh in Canada. Whut u think?" Cleo asked.

"I think that would make me the happiest man on earth!" TJ responded with a huge smile, then picked her up off the ground and spun her around.

Cleo squealed like a child on a swing "Stop, ya gonna mek me dizzy."

Putting her back down on the ground, TJ stated. "I have a request. Come to my birthday party tomorrow. I want you to meet my family. You can just come home with my Aunt Annie when she leaves work tomorrow."

Aunt Annie? Who knew that my little Cleo had stumbled upon my golden ticket to finding John and Marie? Helena thought. She was getting giddy at the thought of crashing that birthday party. She was finally about to exact her revenge. Helena hurried back to the house to make sure that Cleo didn't see her. She had much to do. Her pseudo son's birthday party was tomorrow, but he wasn't the only one in for a surprise!

Cleo happily accepted his invitation and kissed TJ goodbye. She had to figure out a way to sneak out tomorrow without Helena becoming suspicious. Cleo knew that she had not been fulfilling Helena's purpose for her being in Canada, but she was discovering her own.

Cleo snuck back into the house and crept up to bed. Helena pretended that she didn't hear her. Cleo knew that Helena was going to give her some excuse to leave out tomorrow to go to the party, but Cleo needn't think too hard because this was the break for which Helena had been waiting. She was going to make sure that Cleo attended that party, Cleo just didn't know that Helena was going to be her plus one!

That night Cleo and Helena were both too excited to sleep, but for two very different reasons. Cleo was thinking about how much TJ had already become a part of her heart and how she couldn't wait to meet his family and share his special day. Helena couldn't wait to find his family and destroy them.

Chapter Nineteen

Birthday Surprise, Lifetime of Lies

The next day, Cleo woke early and helped Annie with the household chores. She waited on Helena hand and foot and tried her best to stay on her good side. Cleo wanted to do everything possible to be able to attend TJ's birthday party. She had butterflies in her stomach since the moment he asked her to come.

Although Cleo didn't have any money to buy him a gift, she was an excellent seamstress. Cleo asked Annie to help her gather scraps of fabric and to get her a needle and thread. Annie complied, and Cleo had spent the entire night sewing a beautiful scarf and matching gloves to help TJ through those cold Canadian winters. She wrapped the gift in colorful paper and tied it with a ribbon.

Helena had been working on a little gift of her own, for both boys. She had written birthday letters to each boy on the most elegant stationery and sealed it in a festive envelope. Smiling with glee, Helena imagined the faces of Marie and John when the boys read the contents. She could only hope that the shock would kill Marie. That would be the ultimate gift!

As Annie's shift was ending, she was packing her things to prepare to leave. Cleo made up a story about helping Annie make some alterations on some clothing for the Dumas'. Helena knew she was lying, but she agreed to Cleo's request. Trying to hide her excitement, Cleo grabbed her gift and hid it in her coat, then left with Annie. A short time afterward, Helena exited as well. She followed a safe distance behind the young women, so they would not notice that she was following them. They did not see Helena because they were so absorbed in their conversation about TJ and his birthday.

As they reached the street, Helena looked around and wondered which house was theirs. When they arrived at what was a lovely, but modest home with an emerald, green door, Helena thought, *behind this door painted one of my favorite colors, is one of my least favorite people. I can't wait to see my old childhood friends again, but this time I am not playing games in the backyard, I am here for payback!*

Annie and Cleo entered the house, and Annie introduced her to the family.

"Hey everyone, this is the new friend I told you about, Cleo," Annie stated.

"Hi Cleo," everyone said in Unison.

"Nice to meet you, Cleo, I am TJ's mother Marie. Come on in."

"Nice ta meet ya too," Cleo replied.

"Hello Cleo, I am John Devereux, TJ's stepfather and this is his stepbrother John Jr. who is also celebrating a birthday today," John said shaking Cleo's hand.

Hearing the names *John Devereux and John Jr.*, made the smile on Cleo's face fade into a look of pure terror.

Noticing the change in Cleo's demeanor once she heard his name, John asked: "Are you ok my dear?"

Before Cleo even had time to fully process that the family that Helena had come to destroy, was the family of the man she loved, or formulate an answer to John's question, there was a knock at the door. Everyone in the room got quiet. They looked at the door and then at Cleo. Cleo's heart stopped as the door opened, and Helena was standing there.

Without being invited in, Helena made her way through the door. "My, you all do not look happy to see me. I just know you were not planning to celebrate my son's 18th birthday without me, so I am going to assume my invitation got lost in the mail." Helena smirked.

Managing to find the words lodged in his throat, John asked "Helena what the hell are you doing here? When did you get out of the mental hospital and how did you know where to find us? What do you want?"

"So many questions. Which one do I answer first? Let me see; I am here to celebrate my son's 18th birthday. I got out a couple of months ago. I asked around and found out your whereabouts when you divorced me while I was lying helpless in the hospital. And I want to give my son and his brother, a birthday gift." Helena said with a sinister grin.

"We don't want anything from you, now take your gift and leave," John said.

"Oh darling, these gifts are not for you to refuse. They are for the boys", she said as she handed TJ his envelope and asked that he read it aloud.

TJ opened the envelope and read the letter aloud as requested. *"There once was a boy who was born a slave; his father a war hero and very brave. His mother a devoted wife and loyal maid; but these were lies that were all well laid. The truth is a dark tale I'm afraid; and once you know, you'll feel betrayed. Your birth, a result of master and slave; a secret your father took to his grave. Your mother is the one you already know, but your father is none other than John Devereux!"*

TJ looks shocked, then embarrassed, then slowly the pain took hold. Looking at the pain and confusion on TJ's face Marie's heart began to break.

Peter said, "Helena I always knew you were a miserable excuse for a human being, but this is low even for you!"

"Now, now Father Devereux that is no way to talk to your daughter in law. After all, I was locked away in a looney bin for the past nine years, and none of you even thought to check on me! While my husband fled to Canada with his nigger whore!" Helena yelled, then she regained her composure, brushed her red hair away from her face, and straightened her dress before continuing. "Now let's not be rude, its time for my "son" to open his birthday gift," Helena stated handing John Jr. the other envelope.

Marie rushed over and fell at Helena's feet and begged "Helena, please stop this. If you want to punish someone, punish me, not the boys!"

But Marie's pleas fell on deaf ears. Helena had dreamed of this day, and there was no way she was going to stop now.

"My dear Marie, whatever are you afraid of? Let my son open his gift. Sorry, I didn't get you and John a wedding present, but I just didn't know where to find ex-slave and ex-master monogrammed gift sets." Helena said with a smirk.

John Jr. felt a sinking feeling in the pit of his stomach as he opened his letter written in the same nursery rhyme fashion as TJ's. He also read his aloud as requested. *"A boy, born on the day of another; whose status was above all others. Thought a wealthy socialite was his mother, but the truth he would soon uncover. The son of the slave master had a slave for a mother. These lies kept deeply undercover; as well as the fact that he had a twin brother!"*

After John Jr. finished reading, Helena yelled "Surprise!" and threw confetti in the air that she had tucked away in her dress pocket.

The room fell silent as Helena's words began to sink in. Noticing the confused look on the boys' faces, Helena Chimed in again with a laugh, "I know this is a lot to take in boys so let me enlighten you. You two are twins that were born from an unnatural affair between your privileged White father over there and your nigger whore of a mother."

Enthralled in her revenge, Helena didn't see Sarah standing within striking distance. Suddenly, Helena felt a sharp sting across her face and a slight ringing in her ears as she caught herself before hitting the floor. She looked up in shock to Sarah staring down at her.

Helena held her face and shouted "You, insolent slave! How dare you raise a hand to me! I will have you hanged for this!"

Helena received another strike across her face, this time causing her mouth to fill with blood as Sarah responded "You, miserable wench! I have waited decades to draw blood from your filthy lips. We are not in the south dear, and this is not a plantation. We are free, and that means that I am free to beat the very breath out of your body; and if you don't refrain from speaking about my daughter with disrespect, I will do just that. Try me!"

Realizing that she was outnumbered and feeling she had made her point, Helena did not reference Marie again. Marie sat on the floor with her eyes cast down and filling with tears as she prepared herself to answer the questions she knew were coming.

When Dark Secrets Come to Light

It seemed like an eternity passed in silence. The secret that began so long ago was finally out in the open, and it felt as if the entire room was now holding its breath waiting to see what happens next.

John Jr. was the first to speak, and when he did, he aimed his questions at Marie, who was still on the floor seemingly unable to move.

"How can we be twins? We are not the same color. TJ is Black, and I am White. How can this be true? Why would you lie to me my entire life and tell me that someone else was my mother? Did you not want me?" John Jr. asked as the truth ripped through the fabric of everything he had ever known.

"Oh baby, I wanted you more than life itself!" Marie sobbed.

"Then why did you give me away?" John Jr. asked.

Feeling ashamed of the devastation he had caused in the name of greed, Peter interrupted. "It was my fault son. I gave your mother no choice. Helena could not have children, and I needed an heir. When Marie unexpectedly gave birth to twins, and I saw that you had the fair complexion of your father, I made an incorrigible decision to take you from your mother and have you raised as Helena's child. There are no words that I can ever say to excuse my actions or express how deeply sorry I am for making them."

"You should be sorry! How could you do something like that?" John Jr. screamed through tears of anger and hurt.

"Don't be too hard on your grandfather son, I went along with it," John interjected.

"Oh, I see, you viewed my mother as chattel, so her body and her children were yours to do what you like! Is that it?" John Jr. exclaimed then turned to Marie and asked, "How could you fall in love with a man who viewed you as property?"

Putting his arms around his son's shoulders, John responded. "No son, I loved your mother with all my heart. She was and still is the love of my life. I went along with my father's plan because it afforded me the opportunity to at least raise one of my sons, and shower on you all the love I could not openly show for my other son."

Marie walked over to John Jr. and gently held both his hands in hers. "And although I was devastated at first, and my heart broke for you every day. I found comfort in knowing that your father could raise at least one of my sons and he would be spared the life of slavery."

"And what of my life, mother? Did I not deserve to be spared the existence of a slave? Was I not of the same blood as John Jr.? TJ asked.

Wiping away the flowing tears, Marie held her other son's face in her hands and said "Of course you did baby. I tried my best to give you the best life I could, given the circumstances; and next to your being with your birth father, there was no greater father I could have prayed for you to have than Thomas."

TJ rested his forehead against his mother's forehead and let the tears flow. Out of the corner of his eye, he caught a glimpse of Cleo, still standing there with her gift in hand and a look of anguish on her face. TJ began to piece together the part she played in Helena's little surprise.

"So, what reward did Helena promise you to get you to play games with my heart and lead her to my family? How much was destroying my life worth in ill-gotten fare?" TJ asked intently staring at Cleo.

"Ya have ta know TJ, when I met you in da marketplace, I didn't know you wus who Miss Helena was afta. And when I fount out who ya wus, I was standing right heh in this very spot. I cud not have gon through wit Miss Helena's plan if I knew. I have already loss ma heart to ya and I cudn't hurt ya lak dat. If I had known, I wudda warn ya that she was here and bout her plan. I never told Miss Helena bout ya, but she found out and followed me heh taday. Ya have ta kno my heart is true." Cleo begged.

"Oh yes, little miss Cleo is a clever girl. She would have tried her best to protect you, but I have waited a long time to make you all suffer for the hell I had to endure all these years. Undoubtedly it was at the hands of Sarah, but also the mental anguish of knowing my husband was in love with his slave mistress! Cleo's betrayal will be dealt with once we return home." Helena snapped.

"Well now that you have done what you came to do, why don't you do us all a favor and go on back to New Orleans!" Peter yelled.

"Not quite yet, I still have another present for my darling boy," Helena replied.

"What else could you possibly have left to say, Helena? There are no more secrets you can share that the boys do not already know." Marie asked.

"Well, I am glad you asked Marie darling, I am here to offer John Jr. the keys to the kingdom, my father's business. You see as far as everyone in New Orleans knows, John Jr. is still my son; and my father wants me to bring him back with me to teach him the family business. He can come back to America, his home, and become one of the wealthiest young men in New Orleans." Helena stated.

"It's too dangerous to return to America, if anyone found out that he was passing, his very life could be in danger," John said.

"No one would dare question him because no one would believe that I would go along with pretending that the son of a slave was my son. Meanwhile, he would be able to attend the finest schools and have the world open to him." Helena said.

"No way, now get out of my house!" John shouted.

"I do believe today is John Jr's 18th birthday. So, why don't we let him make up his mind shall we?" Helena replied.

"Think about it John Jr. you don't have to live your life in exile. I am offering you a lifetime opportunity to return to a life of luxury, not live like a pauper." Helena retorted while turning her nose up at John and Marie's modest home. "I leave for New Orleans on a steamboat tomorrow at 8:00 am. There will be a ticket waiting for you at the dock. I hope you can see past your current feelings and take advantage of the opportunity I offered to you."

Helena did a mock bow in farewell and left to return to her host's home, feeling vindicated. Cleo exited as well, but she had a surprise of her own for Helena. When Helena returned to New Orleans tomorrow, Cleo would not be with her. She was going to remain in Canada with the man and freedom she had come to love.

That night, everyone answered all the questions the boys had openly and honestly, even about John's true race. Although no one wanted them to find out the way they had, it was a relief to have it out in the open finally. Marie and John were both dreaming of being able to fully embrace both of their twins and their new life in Canada, but little did they know, John Jr. was thinking about Helena's offer.

The next morning, the family awoke to a note from John Jr.

Dear Mom and Dad,

Even as I write those words, I am still in disbelief. I want you both to know that I love you very much and I don't want you to think that my decision to leave means that I love you any less. It is just a lot to take in, and I don't believe that my mind can fully process it. I also don't trust that I can live my life as a Black man. I don't know how.

I have spent my entire life as a White man of privilege. Being White, male and from an affluent family meant that I had no limits on what I could do or when I could do it. Even when we moved to Canada where Blacks had more freedom, I always knew that I didn't HAVE to be there. That I had the privilege to go anywhere I chose.

To have someone tell me that I can no longer do that is not something I am accustomed to, nor do I want to be. Honestly, I feel trapped between two worlds. I know now that I am considered a Black man because of my parentage, but the world sees me, and I see myself as a White man.

Mother, please don't be disappointed in me; I am not as brave as you, I don't have the inner strength to face everything that being Black means today. I cannot live trapped between two worlds, too light to be accepted as a real Black man and shunned from the only world I have ever known.

Although I detest Helena for what she did to you and the rest of my family, I cannot let my hatred of her cloud my judgment and make me miss a great opportunity. She is offering me the chance to be the sole heir to both the Devereux and Marchand fortunes. That is more than anyone can dream.

I know I will come back and visit you someday, but as for now, I must go back to the life I left *behind. I hope that you can both understand. Tell everyone else that I love them as well and I could not ask for a better family.*

Love
John Jr.

After finally having her family all together, Marie lost her son all over again. She hoped that he would be safe, she wondered if she would ever see him again and what type of man he would become under Helena and her parent's influence. With a broken heart, Marie lay down on the bed where her son usually slept, smelling his scent on his pillow and bathing it in her tears.

In the Still of the Night

When Helena left John and Marie's home, she was as giddy as a child on Christmas morning. The thought of the devastation she had caused in their happy little family gave her a feeling of delight. She walked back to her host family's home with a spring in her step and a sinister smile that ran chills down Cleo's spine.

In that instant, she understood why Sarah had placed the spell on Helena all those years ago; and why her cousin Suzanne had such a difficult time finding someone to help her remove it. Helena was a miserable human being, and Cleo instantly regretted the day she ever asked her grandmother to help her. She deserved every torturous night that she endured all those years, and then some.

Cleo walked in silence while Helena rejoiced in accomplishing her objective. They arrived back at the Dumas house just in time for dinner. Helena went upstairs to freshen up, then went downstairs to join her hosts in the dining room. Cleo went to her room to process how a day she was excited about just an hour ago had turned into the worst day of her life. Being around Helena had begun to turn her stomach, so she had no desire to eat anything (not that she would have eaten at the table with the family anyway).

"Good evening everyone. Everything looks so good; and I am positively ravenous." Helena stated as she entered the room carrying a gift for her hosts. Feeling like celebrating, Helena presented the Dumas' with an expensive bottle of Champagne.

"I picked this up in the market today, as a little thank you for your wonderful hospitality during my stay," Helena stated handing the bottle to Mr. Dumas.

"Are you leaving us so soon my dear?" Mrs. Dumas asked.

"Yes, I am afraid I must bid you farewell. I have enjoyed my stay immensely in your fair country, but I have much business to attend to back home, so Cleo and I will be returning to New Orleans tomorrow morning." Helena replied.

"Oh well, in that case, let us open this thoughtful gift and celebrate your last night in Canada." Mr. Dumas stated, ordering one of the servants to open the bottle and serve the table.

"Helena, how did you enjoy your stay? Did you get a chance to do some site seeing or catch a show?" Mrs. Dumas asked.

"Oh yes ma'am, I was entertained while I was here. I saw everything I came to see." Helena responded taking a sip of the champagne with a slight smirk.

Cleo was in her room listening to everything going on in the dining room. She knew that she was not going back to New Orleans with Helena, now she just had to figure out where to live while she tried to establish herself in Canada.

After dinner was over and Helena had sufficiently toasted to her successful journey, she bid her host family goodnight.

"Well, it has been a lovely dinner, but I really must get some sleep. I have a very early boat to catch in the morning." Helena said.

"Alright dear, sleep well." Mrs. Dumas replied.

"And do tell your parents we said hello and how lovely it was to have you visit us." Mr. Dumas stated.

"I will do just that. You were the perfect hosts, and I do so appreciate your hospitality. Goodnight." Helena replied. Then exited upstairs to her bedroom.

I know Marie is not sleeping peacefully tonight! Helena thought as she prepared for bed. After she had dressed in her bedclothes, Helena climbed under the covers where she rejoiced in that thought until she drifted off to sleep.

Cleo did not have a peaceful sleep. In fact, she lay awake all-night thinking of the pain that she saw in TJ's face; and the look of betrayal that she saw in his eyes when he looked at her. It broke her heart to know that inadvertently, she was the means Helena used to locate TJ's family; and that she stood there helpless as she watched Helena lay waste to everything he and his brother John Jr. knew about their parents and who they were. The thought made her feel physically ill. Cleo knew she had to convince TJ and his family that it was not her intention to hurt them; but to do that, she had to find a way to stay.

The next morning Helena woke refreshed and ready to make her journey home. Canada had served her purpose, now she was prepared to go back to America. After she scanned the room for any forgotten items, she went to the dock.

"Cleo, get my bags. We must leave at once to make the morning steamboat home." Helena barked.

When Cleo descended the stairs with her bags in hand, she didn't know where she was going to end up that day or where she was going to sleep that night. She did know she would rather sleep on the streets of Canada than in her old bed at the Marchand plantation.

Cleo placed both hers and Helena's bags into the carriage to go to the dock. When they both climbed in and settled in their seats, Helena caught a glimpse of Cleo staring at her. Noticing the obviously disapproving look on Cleo's face, Helena asked: "Is there something you would like to share?"

Cleo did not hesitate to respond to Helena's question. She knew that she was not going back to New Orleans and that Helena could not force her to.

"I don' unastan how ya cud be so happy hurting people lak dat. But I am beginning ta see why Mr. John lef ya fa Miss Marie." Cleo stated.

Becoming infuriated that Cleo would dare speak to her that way Helena reached over and smacked Cleo across the face. "Just who do you think you are talking to, girl? How dare you speak to me that way? I am your mistress!" Helena barked, then settled back into her seat straightening her clothing and feeling that she had reminded Cleo of her place and quashed any further insubordinate comments.

Cleo held her face and gave Helena a stare that made her blood run cold.

"Dat's da las time you gon' hit me. Ya shud be caful, Ms. Sarah ain't da only one dat can make ya nightmare come true." Cleo said in a slow, deliberate tone.

Helena's entitled smile left her face, replaced with a look of fear. They rode in silence until they got to the dock. When they arrived, Helena was happy to see that John Jr. was there waiting for her. She pushed the uneasiness of the last few moments with Cleo to the back of her mind and got out to greet him.

"Well, I am pleasantly surprised to see you son. Did you pick up your ticket? Helena quizzed.

"Yes, I did "mother." John Jr. replied.

"Excellent! Let's prepare to depart." Helena said motioning for Cleo to retrieve her bags.

When Helena saw that Cleo was standing there with only her bag in her hand, but was making no effort to retrieve Helena's, she snapped. "Cleo. Get my bag, so that we can go home!"

In a defiant stance, Cleo responded. "I am home." Then turned and started to walk away.

"Just where do you think you are going, you insolent little girl? You belong to me!" Helena yelled.

Stopping in her tracks but never turning around, Cleo responded. "I belong to no one." Then she continued to walk away. Cleo didn't know what to do next, so she sat down on the bench at the dock to collect her thoughts. She didn't know what she was going to say to TJ or his family, but she knew it had to be something. Cleo had never met anyone like TJ before, and she was not about to let him go that easily.

Chapter Twenty-Two

The Aftermath

The house felt cold and silent the day after Helena's surprise visit. Just like a hurricane, she had blown through their lives once again and turned it upside down. Leaving broken pieces of what used to be valuable and sacred discarded like garbage. There were no words that could describe the pain Marie was going through nor anything anyone could do to help ease her pain. It was as if her life was to be one of constant mourning for the son who was taken from her all those years ago.

At least when he was growing up, she was able to see him every day, have a hand in raising him and watch him grow and experience life. It was a strange twist of fate that although she, her husband and both of her children were all the same race, the difference in their complexion put them in different classes.

She could not begrudge her son for taking advantage of using this difference to live a better life. Who would choose a life of torment, unfair treatment and living under the constant threat of death, when merely playing the part society sees allows him to live like royalty, with respect and power.

As Marie sat on the edge of her son's bed in quiet contemplation, John entered the room. He felt as if all the pain in Marie's life was because she loved him. John was the reason that Helena hated and tortured her; John was also the reason their son chose to live as a White man because he couldn't face life a Black one. John and John Jr. had the luxury of existing in whatever world they chose, Marie and TJ could not shed their identities so easily. How could John condemn his son for not admitting that he was Black when he still had not. Being at a loss for words, John decided to just sit beside her in quiet reflection.

There was a soft knock at the door, and Sarah appeared carrying a tray of food. "How are you feeling baby? Do you want to try to eat something?' Sarah asked.

"I can't eat mama. I can't move. I feel like if I move from this spot, I am going to fall apart. I don't know how to move on from this. I don't know how to start putting the pieces of my life back together again. How do I do that mama? Marie questioned.

"One piece at a time baby, one piece at a time," Sarah replied.

Seeing how fragile her daughter was, there was no way that Sarah was going back home. She had no reason to go back. Her children and one of her grandchildren were in Canada. She had a new daughter-in-law and son-in-law here as well, and she and her husband can live a better quality of life. As far as Sarah was concerned, they were now Canadians.

"You have to try to eat, baby girl so you can keep up your strength. Don't forget you still have another son and a husband that needs you." Sarah said, leaving the tray on the table and giving them some privacy.

Sarah went to check on the rest of the family and found TJ sitting at the kitchen table with Cleo's gift in hand.

"Well, are you going to open it?" Sarah asked.

"Why should I? It was a duplicitous person who led the monster who wanted to destroy my family to our doorstep. I cannot think of anything she could give me at this point that I could have a use for."

"Duplicitous? Well, now that's a strong word for a little girl who I believe had no idea who you were until right before your father introduced himself and your brother." Sarah stated.

"Grandma, you may believe that, but she came here to help Helena destroy us. That is unforgivable" TJ snapped.

"Baby, you don't want to go down that path of holding grudges, because you become a prisoner of your own unforgiving heart; and you miss out on what I believe is an opportunity to share your life with someone that makes you happy. Don't let your foolish pride rob you of that." Sarah said.

TJ opened the gift and saw the handmade scarf and gloves and a smile came over his face. He knew Cleo didn't have any money, so the fact that she went through the trouble of making him such a thoughtful gift touched his heart.

"A handmade scarf and gloves set, how nice. At least you will have something to keep you warm, because a cold heart certainly will not." Sarah said and exited the room.

TJ knew that his grandmother was right, he only hoped that he was able to catch Cleo before she boarded that boat and returned with Helena to New Orleans. TJ put on his gloves and scarf and grabbed his coat. He headed to the boat dock in hopes that he had not allowed his foolish pride to cause him to lose someone he had grown to care about genuinely.

When he arrived, he asked the dock manager if the boat to America had already left, to which the manager replied that it had. Feeling disappointed and hurt, he turned to leave, then he saw Cleo sitting on the bench.

"You stayed here, why?" TJ stated,

"Yes, I did. Dere ain't nothing fa me in New Orleans, and I was hoping I could continue to learn more about this wonderful place." Cleo said.

"Now that Helena is gone, where will you stay?" TJ asked.

"Don know yet, but I know I wud rather sleep on da streets in Canada, then in a bed in the Marchand house," Cleo replied.

"Well what kind of gentlemen would I be, If I let you do that?" TJ smiled then continued. "I think we may be able to make room for you at my house."

Cleo jumped up and threw her arms around TJ's neck, then kissed him softly on the lips before grabbing her things to follow him back to his home. Cleo knew at that moment she made the right choice.

When they arrived back at the house, Sarah had a big breakfast already prepared and on the table. The home was warm, yet there was still a slight chill in the air. Cleo knew it wasn't because of the presence of cold weather, but the absence of a piece of their family.

Cleo put her bags down and greeted the family. She attempted to offer her apologies again for what Helena had done, but Sarah interrupted her by giving her a warm embrace.

"Shh. Hush now chile. You don't owe us any apologies. We know that Helena used you to get to us. I can read people very well. I knew from the very moment I met you that you had a good heart, and that heart belonged to my grandson. I also sensed that you had an energy that only someone like me would pick up. Someone has trained you. Was it your mother?" Sarah inquired.

Amazed at how accurately Sarah was able to read her, Cleo responded "No ma'am. It was my grandma, Sadie. She worked fa the Marchand's ever since Helena was a baby. She raised her."

"Ah, so she was the one that broke my spell. Maybe she knew a side of Helena we never knew that endeared her to your grandma." Sarah stated.

Shaking her head, Cleo responded quickly, "No ma'am. She thought Helena was an evil person. She knew Helena was hexed from the beginnin' she jus neva hepped her befo' now".

"So why did she help her now?" Sarah quizzed.

"I hurd Helena's cousin, Ms. Suzanne, crying one day 'bout how no one would hep break the hex an old woman in the bayou said was on Helena. So, I tol' her dat my grandma Sadie cud hep her and I took her to see her. My grandma still didn't want ta hep her; and she wadn't dat happy dat I let Ms. Suzanne know dat she even knew how ta hep Helena. She only did it 'cause Ms. Suzanne begged her ta hep her, and she loved Ms. Suzanne lak, a daughter. Said she raised her up with Helena, but she wuddn't nuthin lak Helena. Ms. Suzanne had always loved and respected my grandma, so she hepped her." Cleo explained.

"I see. Where is your grandma now? Won't she expect you to come home?" Sarah quizzed.

"No, ma'am. My grandma went to the bayou to live out her las days wit her family. She didn't want me to get trapped jus workin at da Marchand's. She wanted me ta find my way. An when I came heh, I felt lak I started to find my way for the furs time, I am jus sorry it caused so much pain." Cleo professed.

"Well, what is done, is done now. We have to all move forward from here. I just hate that I lost my grandson to that viper. But enough about that. Put your bag down chile and get yourself some breakfast. You are among family now, and this family always takes care of its own." Sarah said.

Motherless Child

The Steamboat pulled away from the dock; and suddenly Helena and John Jr. were thrust into this awkward silence that was deafening. Helena had been so preoccupied with her plan to steal John Jr. from Marie and exact her revenge; she never thought about what would happen once she had him.

Helena and John Jr. were virtual strangers. They had not seen each other since he was eight years old. Helena had left him and went to New Orleans. She was institutionalized for nine years shortly after her arrival in New Orleans, and they had no contact during that time. Even when Helena was there during John Jr's childhood, she wasn't the one raising him; that had always been Marie's job.

Now that they were alone, and the dust was beginning to settle, Helena faced the realization that she had no idea how to be a parent to John Jr.; and worse than that, knowing that he didn't want her to in the first place.

Since there was no real maternal bond between them, there was nothing to bridge the gap that time and distance had created. Faced with the long journey ahead of them, Helena tried to engage John Jr. in conversation to help pass the time.

"So, what have you been doing here in Canada?" Helena asked.

Turning away from the window that he had been staring out of since he took his seat, John Jr. responded "TJ, and I were attending school. He has dreams of being a lawyer and fighting for the rights of Black people. I hadn't quite figured out my path in life yet, but I was leaning towards becoming a businessman. I even…"

"School? They allowed him to attend school with Whites?" Helena interrupted with disdain.

John Jr. stopped mid-sentence and stared at Helena for a moment. The look was enough that she quickly tried to change the subject.

"So why did you come to Canada in the first place?" Helena asked after clearing her throat.

John Jr. continued to stare at her a few more moments, making Helena visibly uncomfortable, before answering.

"After you left for New Orleans, Grandpa Peter had heard some stories about how dangerous things were getting in America, especially in the south. He arranged for my father and Ms. Marie…" John Jr. stopped speaking suddenly. It was if the words had gotten stuck in his throat after he spoke Marie's name.

"Are you ok, son?" Helena asked, snapping John Jr. out of the trance that he temporarily slipped in to.

"Yes, I just haven't spoken her name since I found out that she was my mother and that TJ, and I are twins. It's still a lot to process." he replied.

Allowing her hatred and arrogance to get in the way of her thinking once again, Helena quipped, "That's fine by me; I don't care if I ever hear her name again. Now that the spell is finally broken that wench's mother put on me, I am free and have come to rescue you. You can put all of those awful people behind you son; your mother is here now…"

Slamming his hand down on the seat beside Helena, John Jr. retorted "Don't you ever talk about them, you hear me?" As long as you have breath in that vile body of yours, don't you ever talk about any of them in my presence!"

"John Jr! Is that any way to speak to your mother?" Helena asked in astonishment.

With a look she had seen in his father and grandfather's eyes many times before, John Jr. spat back "I HAVE NO MOTHER!"

Nervously looking around to see how many people's attention his little outburst had captured, Helena stated, "I am still your mother John Jr. I have cared for you as my own since your birth, and the entire time I was locked away in that god-awful place all I could do was think about you. I wondered how you were and if you knew what had happened to me and if you did, why had you not come to look for me? All I wanted to do was get out of there and come back and see my darling boy."

With a sinister laugh, John Jr. quizzed. "Is that so? Well, if that is the case, why did you leave me in the first place? You were locked away once you left and went to New Orleans. You knew that things were so dangerous during that time, why would you leave your child and run away?"

Stammering to find her words Helena sat with her mouth open, but no words could find their way out.

Finally, John Jr. answered for her. "Let me help you "mother," you left because you have never cared one little bit what happened to me. You knew the entire time who I was and who my parents were. You despised my birth mother, and you only took me as your son, because you knew it would hurt her. You despised me, because every time you looked at me, I was a reminder that your husband loved a slave and hated you. I was a constant reminder that even with all your class and breeding, she could still do something you could not...produce an heir. You knew that you would be looked at as a failure by everyone, including your father if you didn't produce the heir that everyone expected. So, you saw me as a way for you to salvage your pride if no one knew my true parentage. Isn't that right mother dear?"

Helena sat there at a loss for words, so John Jr. continued, "Don't worry; I don't want you to waste your breath trying to deny it. The way I see it, there has been enough pretending between us, so honesty is a somewhat refreshing change of pace. This time, I am not in the dark about where I come from, I just have to figure out where I am going and who I am going to be in this life. A choice that my complexion affords me and your lineage entitles me. Pretending to be your son, I know that I can open doors that would not be open to me otherwise. But make no mistake, you were never and will never be my mother. You are just a way for me to live the best life possible, and I am a way to give your father what he wants more than anything, an heir to mold in his image. As long as we are clear on that and you keep my family's name from crossing your miserable lips, we will get along fine."

And with that, John Jr. sat back in his seat and resumed watching the scenery pass. He missed his family he was leaving behind. Especially now that he knew that the feelings of connectedness he felt for Marie and TJ were not a symptom of them being around him, but of them being a part of him.

John Jr. did not know if he would ever return to Canada; in fact, he didn't know where he belonged. He felt trapped between two worlds and yet he didn't completely have a connection to either. Even though he had two mothers, one of birth and the other of convenience, at that moment, he felt like a motherless child.

Helena and John Jr. spent the remainder of their trip in silence. Helena read a book that she had brought along for the journey; and John Jr. tried to figure out what he was going to do when he got to New Orleans. He was just getting accustomed to his new life in Canada, and now he was returning to his old life in America. Although he was back in the country of his birth, the rules were different now. He was no longer a White man born into a position of privilege; he was a Black man trying to pass for the very race that made him hide in the first place.

Back to Business

Although their family reunion was short-lived, it was beautiful to have everyone under one roof again. They came to warn their children that Helena was on the way to start trouble, but in the end, she still accomplished her objective. Now, everyone was trying to pick up the pieces and figure out where they were going to go from here.

"Good morning everyone," Peter stated as he entered the kitchen.

Sarah was already up cooking breakfast, and Nate was helping her by setting the table.

"Good Morning" they both replied in a somber unison.

Peter noticed that he didn't see Marie or John anywhere. "Where are John and Marie? Are they still sleeping? I thought I was the last one to rise this morning" Peter inquired while pouring himself a cup of coffee.

Just as he was about to sit down at the table, he noticed John emerging from the bedroom looking sullen. He murmured a good morning to everyone and then sat down beside his father. Sarah placed a cup of coffee in front of him and stated, "Here. It looks like you could use this."

"Thank you, Sarah," John replied taking a drink from the cup.

"Where is Marie?" Peter asked.

"She refuses to get out of bed. Ever since that she-devil Helena came to town and stole our son away from us, Marie has withdrawn into a depressed state. She won't eat, she barely sleeps, and when she does sleep, she tosses and turns until she wakes in fits of crying." John replied.

"My poor baby. Just when it seemed she had finally found happiness and escaped Helena's talons, her heart is ripped right out of her chest, all over again." Sarah said

"Nah, Nah, hummingbird. Don' git yo'sef all worked up again. Marie gon be aw'right. She strong lak her mama." Nate assured Sarah.

"I hope you right Nate. It breaks my heart to see her like this." Sarah said, with her eyes welling with tears.

"Nate is right Sarah, you raised a strong young woman, and that is one of the things Helena always envied about her. No matter what unspeakable act Helena committed trying to break her spirit, she never could." Peter stated.

"Thank you both for trying to reassure me, but it is Marie that needs the reassurance now. She needs assurance that she will see her son again, and unfortunately, that is something none of us can honestly do." Sarah responded.

The door opened, and TJ walked into the house. He had been out with Cleo getting her enrolled in school since early that morning. Jacob and Annie had offered to let her stay with them until she graduated. "Good Morning everyone. TJ said as he walked into the kitchen to greet his family.

"Good morning baby. You were up early this morning." Sarah replied.

"Yes, ma'am. I had to go over to Uncle Jacob's to pick up Cleo and take her over to my school. She never had the opportunity to get a formal education, so I wanted to help her get enrolled." TJ responded.

"That's great son. She seems like a fine young lady. I am happy that she decided to stay in Canada." John said.

"Me too. Where is my mother? She is not up yet?" TJ asked.

"No son. She ain't. Yo mamma, not feelin'gud. She ain't lef dat room since John Jr. lef." Nate answered.

"This can't go on any longer," TJ said as he rose to leave.

"Where are you going, baby?" Sarah asked.

"To get my mother back," TJ replied, and he grabbed his coat and headed out the door.

Everyone looked at each other bewildered, but hopeful that where ever TJ was going, he could bring back something to help Marie.

TJ knocked on the office door of Dr. Abigail Wise. Dr. Wise was a guest lecturer in one of TJ's classes, and she also worked as a medical doctor with her practice.

"Yes? How can I help you?" Dr. Wise stated, not looking up from her desk.

"Sorry to disturb you Dr. Wise, but I need your help" TJ stated.

Dr. Wise was the product of a Black mother and a White father. She was an attractive older woman with slightly greying hair, slim frame, and fair complexion. Even though someone of her appearance could easily pass for White, Dr. Wise was proud of her Black ancestry and refused to do so. She always informed anyone who questioned her that she was a Black woman.

Dr. Wise looked up and saw TJ standing there, and she responded: "TJ, come on in; what can I do for you?"

"It's my mother. Ever since my twin brother left, she has been depressed. She won't eat, can't sleep; and she won't get out of bed. I am afraid if you don't help her, I am going to lose my mother as well as my brother." TJ urged.

"I wasn't even aware that you had a twin brother." Dr. Wise replied.

"It's a long story, that I will share with you along the way, but I need you to help my mother. I have never seen her like this, and everyone in my family is at their wit's end trying to figure out how to reach her. TJ responded.

"Oh dear. I will do my best, but first I must examine your mother. Let me grab my doctor's bag, and you can lead the way." Dr. Wise stated.

After a short walk, TJ and the doctor arrived at TJ's house. He had filled Dr. Wise in on the details as they walked, so she was already up to speed upon their arrival.

"Everyone. I would like you meet Dr. Wise. I met her when she was a guest lecturer in my class. I brought her here to help mama." TJ stated.

"How exactly is your professor going to help your mama? She doesn't need any homework. She needs someone who can help her get over her heartbreak." Peter quipped.

"I am also a medical doctor sir; now if you all will excuse me, I would like to get a look at my patient." Dr. Wise replied.

"By all means doctor; please see if you can help my little girl." Sarah pleaded.

"I will do my best ma'am" Dr. Wise responded, then followed TJ to Marie's room.

Something about this beautiful woman intrigued Peter. He was used to beautiful women, they were a dime a dozen, but this woman was not only beautiful, she was also smart and confident. For the first time since he lost his darling Elizabeth, someone genuinely peaked his interest; maybe because she reminded him of her. Whatever the reason that caught Peter's attention, he planned to get to know more about the beautiful doctor.

TJ knocked on the door to Marie's bedroom. "Mama, I have someone with me that would like to talk to you for a little while, her name is Dr. Wise. She is a professor and doctor. I thought she might help you feel better. TJ said.

Marie did not even turn around. "I don't want to talk to anyone, TJ. Just leave me alone and let me rest." Marie replied.

"Mama, I know John Jr. is gone, but I am your son as well, and I am still here! You have to stop acting like both of your children are gone!" TJ screamed.

"Settle down TJ, yelling is not going to help her. Maybe it would be best if you left me alone with your mother so that we can have a little chat." Dr. Wise suggested.

TJ reluctantly left the room to rejoin his family in the living room. He knew they were anxious to hear what the doctor thought about Marie's condition.

"So, what did the doc say?" Peter asked.

"Nothing yet, she asked me to leave the room, so she could talk to mama alone. She thought my presence was not helpful." TJ said solemnly.

"I'm sure the doctor knows what she is doing sweetheart, and she just wants what is best for your mother," Sarah assured.

Back in the room, the doctor evaluated Marie. After about 20 minutes, the doctor emerged to fill the family in on her diagnosis.

"Marie is depressed. She is going through a sort of grieving process with the loss of her son. I have prescribed her with some opiates to help her sleep, but I will also check on her throughout the week to help her through this process." Dr. Wise offered.

"Whut can we do ta hep doc?" Nate inquired.

"Be patient with her. Give her lots of love and understanding. Remind her of all the things that she has left to live for." Dr. Wise instructed.

"Thank you, doctor. I will walk you out." Peter offered.

"You are welcome. I will be back to check on Marie in a few days." Dr. Wise responded.

As Peter walked Dr. Wise out, he couldn't help but let her know that she had sparked his interest.

"Dr. Wise. I know this is not the most appropriate time given the reason for your visit, but I have to say, you are one of the most beautiful women that I have ever had the pleasure to meet." Peter stated.

"Why thank you, but I have a feeling I am not the only woman to be exposed to your charms." Dr. Wise replied.

"I have a feeling you are the one woman that is immune to them," Peter stated noticing that Dr. Wise did not swoon over his advances as other women did.

"I am vaccinated, I am a doctor." Dr. Wise quipped.

Beguiled by her beauty and quick wit, Peter was determined to get into her good graces.

"Well, maybe I caught you at the time you need a booster," Peter replied with a devilish smile.

"I am a responsible doctor sir; my vaccines are current. Dr. Wise replied with a smirk.

"Ah, but the lady did bestow a smile upon me; now my day is all the brighter," Peter said with his charming southern drawl.

Peter gazed into Dr. Wise's eyes like a snake charmer hypnotizing a King Cobra; and despite her best attempt, he was penetrating her hard exterior. Attempting to hide her blush, Dr. Wise responded, "Good day Mr. Devereux. I shall return in the morning to check on Marie."

"Then I shall await your arrival as a child does Christmas morning," Peter replied.

Breaking his gaze, Dr. Wise hurried down the street toward her office. Peter watched her as she disappeared. It had been years since anyone has stirred any emotion in Peter, and he was enjoying the feeling. He could not wait to see her again.

Be Careful What You Wish For

Alexander and Oliva Marchand greeted Helena and John Jr. when they arrived in New Orleans.

"John Jr., my boy! Come here and hug your old grandpa! Alexander exclaimed.

"Hey, grandpa." John Jr. replied hugging Alexander.

"Well, don't forget about your grandmother young man, I need one of those hugs as well. Look at you, you are taller than your grandpa now, and you have turned into quite the handsome young man!" Oliva stated hugging him tightly.

"It's good to see you too grandma." John Jr. responded.

"Where is Cleo?" Olivia quizzed.

"She decided to remain in Canada. She said something about there being better opportunities for Black people or something like that. I didn't press her; it's not like she isn't replaceable." Helena stated.

"Oh, I will certainly miss Cleo, she was such a sweet girl, and she did such an excellent job. No one did a better job polishing the silver than she did." Oliva stated.

Alexander nodded his head in agreement, "And no one can clean my study just the way I like it."

"Well, is anyone happy to see me? I mean you are both sitting here lamenting the loss of a servant like she was your daughter and gushing over your long-lost grandson like you found the holy grail. Helena stated feeling a little dejected.

"Well, of course, Helena, but we are just talking about how much Cleo is missed because she was a good worker; and we are gushing over John Jr. because we are excited to see our grandson. It has been ten years since we last saw him. We are still confused as to why he was in Canada in the first place, but I guess we have plenty of time to discuss that. Right now, I just want to get my grandson home and settled in." Alexander replied.

The Marchand's continued to bombard John Jr. with questions on the carriage ride home, but to him, the entire trip was a blur. He saw their lips moving in an excited tone, but all he kept thinking was that he barely knew these people. He missed the family that he had with his parents and brother; but after learning the truth, he felt like he just needed to place as much distance between them as possible.

John Jr. needed to figure out what world he felt most comfortable in; and no matter what, he knew he would have more opportunities as a White man. In fact, a White man was all he knew how to be. Even though he knew he was a Black man, it was a role he was unfamiliar with and wasn't sure he wanted to learn. Besides, his father was a Black man that was still passing for White, so apparently John, Sr. felt the same way as his son.

Feeling as if competing for attention with her pseudo son was futile at this moment, Helena disappeared into her room and didn't bother to engage with her parents or anyone else any further. She was exhausted from the trip and fighting for her parent's acknowledgment. She thought that a nap would refresh her and maybe give her parents time to get adjusted to having their grandson in the house.

Olivia ordered the servants to take John Jr.'s bags to his room. When Olivia learned that her grandson was coming to stay with them, she decked his new room out in grand fashion. Olivia ordered custom linens for his bed and decorated his room with furnishings befitting a young prince. Olivia spared no expense, she had missed out on years of spoiling her only grandchild, and she was going to make up for lost time.

Once John Jr. saw his room and took inventory of his surroundings, he decided he wanted some alone time to process his thoughts. He told everyone that he was tired from the long journey and just wanted to rest. They obliged him and instructed everyone that he was not to be disturbed until supper. He laid down on his plush bed and let his thoughts drift away.

Olivia was busying herself ensuring that the grand feast she had planned to welcome her grandson was cooked to her exact specifications. She ordered the fattest pheasant available with all the trimmings and a custom-made French pastry for dessert. When everything was done, Olivia called everyone down for dinner.

Olivia set John Jr. at the head of the table when he came to dinner; a place usually reserved for Alexander. Since this was a special occasion, Alexander wanted his grandson to sit in his seat. The servants made John Jr.'s plate and his grandparents were so engrossed in his presence that they began to eat before Helena even got to the table. An act she was sure to point out.

"Well, I see you started without me," Helena stated visibly annoyed.

"Oh, Helena darling, we weren't sure you were coming. You seemed so worn out from your journey; and with you just getting out of the hospital, we didn't want to disturb your rest." Oliva explained.

"I am alright, mother, and I wish you and daddy would stop treating me like a fragile doll that is going to crack up at the first sign of stress!" Helena shouted slamming her hands on the table so hard the silverware bounced.

Looking astonished, everyone sat utterly silent for a while, trying to gauge Helena's mental state and her next move. Helena smoothed her hair from her face, straightened out her ruffled dress, then sat down calmly and placed her napkin in her lap. She then sipped her water as if nothing happened, making her parents wonder if maybe Helena came home too soon. Trying to move past her little floor show, her parents decided to change the subject.

"John Jr. I know you just arrived and may want to ease into things, but I would like for you to come to the office with me tomorrow, so I can show you how things work. If you are going to be running the whole operation one day, you may as well start learning now. You think you are up to it?" Alexander asked.

Taking a sip of his water and letting that thought seep in for a moment, John Jr. replied "Sure grandpa. That sounds good."

"That's my boy! No one could doubt you were my grandson; you are Marchand through and through!" Alexander exclaimed patting John Jr. on the back.

Humph! Marchand my Aunt Sally! That boy is no more a Marchand than Cleo; and if you knew that you were about to hand over the keys to the kingdom to a half-breed, you would drop dead right now daddy dearest! Helena thought as she swirled her drink around in her cup.

"Oh, wonderful. I have another surprise for you John Jr. In anticipation of your joining the family business, we made an appointment with our tailor to make you a custom-made suit for your first day and got you a personalized briefcase." Olivia stated.

"That was a nice gesture grandma. Thank you." John Jr. replied.

"Nonsense. You are our grandson, and you will have every comfort befitting a Marchand." Olivia responded.

Helena chugged glass after glass of wine, while she looked on in resentment. John Jr. was settling into his new life quite nicely and was molded in the image of Alexander Marchand himself.

After dinner, John Jr. climbed the massive staircase to his new bedroom. When he opened the door, he remembered the life he had before moving to Canada. All gold accents and custom furniture decorated the room. His bed had the most expensive bedding money could buy, and expensive artwork adorned his walls. His initial reservations about returning to this world started to subside as he enjoyed his new surroundings slowly.

When he climbed into his plush bed that night, John Jr. stared at the ceiling. Although he was reacclimating himself to the lifestyle of the upper echelon, he was still wrestling with some conflicting emotions. He knew that his leaving had an impact on his family, but he was not aware just how much. He also didn't know how to process everything he had recently learned about his identity and from whom he came.

John Jr.'s emotions fluctuated from anger and resentment for being deceived about his parents, to a sense of longing to be back with them. He also felt a strange feeling of relief that Helena was not his biological mother. Even though it meant that he was not the White man he was now pretending to be, the more he learned about Helena, the less he liked her. Now that he was taking over her parent's attention and affection, Helena was starting to dislike John Jr. as well. After tossing and turning for a while, he finally drifted off to sleep.

A Face of Many Colors

The next morning, John Jr. rose early to begin his new life as the Marchand heir. Olivia had given the staff a list of all the things her grandson mentioned that he liked to eat, so his first breakfast in his new home was a lavish buffet of all his favorites.

"Good morning sweetheart, how did you sleep?" Olivia quizzed.

"Like a prince." John Jr. responded as he took his seat at the table.

"You are a prince; my boy and I am the King," Alexander stated with a satisfied smile.

"Yes grandfather, I am aware that you are the king around here and this is your castle. I am excited to learn everything you have to teach me about the business and life in general." John Jr. replied.

"That's my boy! You are the spitting image of me when I was your age. You are going to go far in this life son, and when I am done grooming you, you are going to make a fine successor! I am so glad that your mother finally came to her senses and brought you home. You have been with the Devereuxs your entire life; it's time that you get to know the Marchand side of your family". Alexander stated.

By this time Helena was arriving at the table. She caught her father's heartfelt declaration for his pseudo-grandson and was visibly annoyed.

"Well good morning everyone. I see once again; no one bothered to wake me or wait for me to eat." Helena said placing her napkin in her lap.

"Helena darling, stop being so sensitive. No one is trying to ignore you. Honestly, if I didn't know any better I would swear that you were jealous of your own son!" Olivia exclaimed.

Helena sat back and folded her arms like a five-year-old having a temper tantrum.

"Well, you may not be trying to ignore me, but you most certainly are! Ever since John Jr. got here, you have forgotten all about me, and it's not fair! I have been locked up in the looney bin for almost a decade and not once during all that time did my darling son even attempt to see me, or you for that matter! Now he decides to grace us with his presence, and you two are falling all over yourselves like he is the messiah or something! Helena shouted.

Bam! Alexander slammed his fist down on the table hard enough that the glasses shook, and liquid spilled onto the table.

"That is, it! I have had enough Helena! I am sorry that you had to be committed, but you are home now. I am not going to allow you to keep using your stay in the asylum as an excuse to behave like a petulant child! Now, I think it best that you have your breakfast in your room. Since our presence seems to ignite your unruly behavior, you should spend some time with the only person whose company you appear to be able to stand, your own!" Alexander shouted.

Helena sat there in shock for a few moments. Her father had never yelled at her before or spoken so harshly to her. Helena felt it was all John Jr.'s fault and she began thinking his presence was going to be the new source of her unhappiness. She took her plate and left the table headed to her room while muttering to herself.

"I should have known better than to bring him here! First Marie stole the love of my husband; now her son has taken the love of my parents." She mumbled on her way to her room.

Helena had planned to take John Jr. away from John and Marie to ruin their happy lives; but she soon realized that only life she succeeded in destroying was her own. Helena entered her room, slamming the door behind her. She put the plate on her vanity and then fell across her bed burying her face in the pillow to muffle the sound as she screamed from frustration.

Meanwhile, downstairs everyone resumed their breakfast and prepared to start their day.

"I apologize, son; your mother apparently is still not well. We have tried to be patient with her, because of the ordeal she went through, but that is no excuse for her behavior." Alexander offered.

"It's ok grandpa; I don't take it personally. We just have to keep her in our prayers." John Jr. responded with feigned concern.

Truthfully, for everything Helena had done to his parents, watching her suffer made John Jr. feel like his being here was also a way to get revenge for the pain she caused his parents.

"Well now, are you ready to see the empire?" Alexander asked.

"I can't wait," John Jr. responded and rose to follow his grandfather out to the waiting carriage.

On their ride, Alexander pointed out all the exciting sites in New Orleans. He educated his grandson on the rich history of the city and on all the buildings that made up the Marchand fortune. When they pulled up to a tailor's shop, John Jr. looked confused.

"Is this one of your businesses?" he asked.

"No son, this is my tailor. He makes all of my suits; now he will make all of yours as well." Alexander responded ushering him out of the carriage and into the shop.

The tailor was already waiting for them and instructed John Jr. to step onto a small, raised platform in front of a mirror. He complied, and the tailor began taking his measurements.

"So how does it feel to be back in New Orleans?" Alexander quizzed.

"It's different. I don't remember being here. I was just a baby when we moved to North Carolina; then we moved to Canada when I was eight-years-old. Even though I know this is where I was born, it is unfamiliar," he responded.

"Well, you have all the time in the world to explore what New Orleans has to offer. You are a

Marchand, so this city is yours. Have fun discovering everything there is to discover." Alexander stated.

John Jr. let that thought sink into his head, and as he looked at himself in the mirror, he began to feel powerful. He remembered what it was like to be a part of the elite, and he was now ready to rejoin those ranks. With a final approving look, he and Alexander bid the tailor goodbye and went back to the carriage.

They rode the remainder of the way to the office in silence. John Jr. was looking out the window and saw a Black man walking down the street. The man was well dressed and looked like he was a man of stature. He was carrying an armful of beautifully wrapped packages. When a White man appearing to be of a low class came down the street in the opposite direction, John Jr. heard the White man shout at the Black man.

"Outta my way nigger!" and knocked the packages out of the Black man's hands.

The Black man just bowed his head and moved out of the White man's way, careful not to make eye contact.

"Sorry sir," said the Black man as he moved out of the White man's way then picked up his now sullied packages.

No one blinked at this occurrence, and no one came to the Black man's aid. John Jr. knew that there was no way that he could live like that, but his heart broke at the thought that if his brother and mother were living in New Orleans that is the life they would live, but he and his father had a choice to live as they chose.

John Jr.'s thoughts were interrupted when they finally arrived at his grandfather's office.

"Ok son, this is it. Let's go." Alexander stated.

John Jr. stepped out of the carriage and walked into the building with his grandfather.

"Good morning Mr. Marchand." A petite young woman stated while taking Alexander's coat and hat.

"Good morning Charlotte. Let me introduce you to my grandson John Devereux, Jr. Please make sure he has everything that he needs. Alexander ordered.

"Yes Sir," She responded taking John Jr.'s hat, and coat as well.

He continued to follow his grandfather down the hallway to an office at the end of the hall. Alexander pushed open the doors that led to a spacious room with an enormous desk that sat in front of a gigantic window.

"This is an impressive office grandpa. You can see the entire city from that window, and this furniture is exquisite," John Jr. stated looking around the office.

"Every piece of furniture in this office is custom made. You like it?" Alexander asked.

"I love it," John Jr. replied still looking around.

"Good. Because this one is yours," Alexander said with a smile.

"Are you serious? I thought this was your office," he stated in amazement.

"No this is your space; my office is down the hall. Come by my office and see me when you get settled in and I will give you a rundown of the company. If you are going to steer the ship, you need to know the course you are sailing." Alexander said.

John Jr. nodded his head and said: "Okay, I can come now."

Smiling, Alexander responded, "I appreciate your enthusiasm son, but have a seat. Try out your new office. Charlotte will take care of you if you need anything and we have plenty of time."

"OK. Thanks. I will," he replied.

Alexander left John Jr. alone to let him enjoy his new office. Once he was alone, he inspected every inch of his new space. Touching every piece to make sure it was real and not a dream. He went over to the window and looked down at the city streets below. He felt like the King of the world and at that moment, all thoughts of his family and Canada moved further to the back of his mind. He rationalized that if he were going to make the most of his new life, he could not focus on his old one.

In the months following his arrival John Jr. learned quickly. With each passing day, he endeared himself more and more to the Marchands and Helena promptly realized she was becoming less and less relevant. Alexander had always wanted a boy, but when Helena was born, Olivia could not have any more children, so he resolved just to spoil his little princess.

Alexander lavished expensive gifts and comforts on Helena her entire life, but the desire for a son never left him. He thought when Helena got married that would at least give him a son-in-law to fill the void, but John wanted no parts of being close to any Marchand. When Alexander learned that Helena had given birth to a son, his hopes rose again, but then Helena and the rest of the Devereuxs moved away to North Carolina.

When Helena returned to New Orleans without her son and apparently without her mind as well, Alexander gave up hope. Now that John Jr. was finally living with them and seemingly eager to step into that space, Alexander was over the moon with joy. John Jr. became his entire focus. Alexander would spare no expense to make him happy. Helena became nothing more than an afterthought, a means by which Alexander got what he wanted, a son.

Second Chance at Life and Love

Fall 1875

Almost one year had passed since Helena and John Jr.'s departure. During that time, Dr. Wise had spent every day nursing Marie back to health; and every night with Peter. Peter and Dr. Wise enjoyed each other's company immensely, and anyone who saw them could tell they were both smitten with each other. They fawned over each other like two teenagers experiencing their first crush. For Peter's family, it was a welcomed sight. No one could remember a time when he had been so happy, but they all agreed it was long overdue.

"Good morning everyone," Peter said with a huge smile.

"Somebody is in a good mood," John said noticing his father's chipper demeanor.

"Well, it's a beautiful morning outside, the birds are singing, and the air is crisp and fresh!" Peter exclaimed.

"You can tell all that without going outside? You just got up," Marie quizzed poking fun at her father-in-law.

"I just know my dear Marie! It's something about Canada that just makes me feel like a new man!" Peter shouted dancing around the kitchen.

"Could it be a certain beautiful Canadian doctor that has you dancing around and walking with an extra spring in your step?" John quizzed.

"Well Abigail certainly does make this old heart skip a few beats," Peter replied.

The thought of Dr. Wise brought an instant smile on Peter's face. He had never met anyone like her before. Typically, Peter could only tolerate the company of whatever lady he saw in short intervals. It was completely different with Dr. Wise. Peter felt as if there were not enough hours in the day to spend with her. He could not remember enjoying the company of any woman this much other than his beloved wife, Elizabeth.

"I am happy for you dad. Mom would want you to be happy. I think she would approve of Dr. Wise. She is not the typical socialite clamoring for attention and status." John stated.

"She reminds me a lot of your mother. I never thought my heart would even allow anyone to get this close to me again. I thought my heart died with your mother," Peter replied.

"Well, I am glad Dr. Wise could give new life to your heart. I know mom is smiling down from heaven, and now that she knows that you are in good hands, she can truly rest in peace," John stated.

"Thank you, son. That means the world to me," Peter said.

Their emotional moment was interrupted by a knock at the door. Marie opened the door to see Dr. Wise standing there with a warm smile.

Marie greeted her as she invited her in "Good morning Dr. Wise, please come on in."

"Marie darling, how are you feeling this morning?" Dr. Wise asked, hugging Marie.

Over the past year, Dr. Wise had become more like part of the family than Marie's doctor. She came over for dinner, and she and Peter had spent countless hours together.

"I am doing better. I am taking it day by day. In the beginning, I could barely go a moment without feeling like the pain was going to consume me and swallow me whole. Then I was taking it second by second, so I guess day by day is an improvement." Marie replied.

"Yes, it certainly is," Dr. Wise responded holding both of Marie's hands in hers.

"Have a seat Dr. Wise, I will get you some coffee," Marie offered.

"Abigail, please. I am no longer treating you. Now I am just stopping by as a friend. And yes, I would love a cup of coffee, thank you." Abigail replied.

"You are welcome, Abigail," Marie said with a smile.

"I knew the sun seemed to shine brighter suddenly. How are you darling?" Peter stated kissing her on the cheek.

"Better now that I am next to you," Abigail replied returning Peter's affections.

Peter and Abigail sat and talked for a while, and Marie and John excused themselves so that they could give them some privacy. Peter moved in close and placed his face next to hers.

"How is it that I get butterflies every time I see you. I am a grown woman, and yet in your presence, I feel like a school girl," Abigail whispered.

"You are not alone. I never thought I was even capable of feeling excited about anyone anymore. I thought those feelings died with my wife, but with you, I feel like a child on Christmas morning, and you are the greatest gift that any man could ask for." Peter confessed.

Abigail blushed. She loved being with Peter. It had been a long time since either of them had someone in their lives that made them feel the chemistry they had with each other.

"Take a walk with me. It looks like a beautiful morning outside, and I want to talk to you about something important," Peter said.

"OK, that sounds ominous. Is everything alright?" Abigail asked, now looking a bit concerned.

"Everything is perfect, and so are you. Now take a walk with me," Peter reassured her.

Without further questioning, Abigail went with Peter to walk around the town and enjoy the crisp morning air. It was Autumn, and the leaves were bright and colorful. It was the perfect backdrop for a romantic walk and for the topic Peter wanted to discuss. When they came upon a bench in a nearby park, Peter led Abigail over by the hand to have a seat. Taking her hands in his, he got to the reason he wanted to talk to her.

"When I came to Canada, I had one intention, to warn my son and daughter-in-law about Helena. I did not expect to meet someone as wonderful as you. Now that I have you in my life, I am not sure how to face my days without you. You are the last person I think of at night and the first thought of my morning. I am not sure what else this life has in store for me, but I know that I do not want to face it without you." Peter professed.

"Peter, what exactly are you saying?" Abigail asked searching his face for answers.

Soon his intention became clear. Peter pulled a small red box from his pocket and proceeded to get down on one knee in front of her. He opened it and took her by the hand.

"Abigail Wise, will you do me the honor of becoming my wife?" Peter asked.

Her eyes filled with tears, and she exclaimed, "Yes!"

Peter rose and picked her up into his arms and gave his new fiancée a long kiss. They embraced for a while and decided to walk back to the house to tell the rest of the family. They walked hand in hand along the city streets, but they were so happy if felt as if they were walking on a cloud.

That evening, everyone came to Marie and John's house for dinner. Once everyone was there and seated, Peter stood and tapped his glass with his fork to get everyone's attention.

"OK everyone, I know you are probably wondering why I asked everyone to come to dinner tonight. Well, it is because I love you all and each one of you is an important part of my life. And as such, I cannot think of anyone else with whom I would want to share my good news." Peter declared.

"Well, what is it, Peter? You got us all in suspense." Sarah quizzed.

"Yeah dad, don't keep us guessing," John asked.

"Alright, Alright I will tell you. Today, I asked the beautiful Dr. Abigail Wise to be my wife, and she said yes." Peter stated.

The entire room erupted in applause, and everyone was excited. The family showered the couple with well wishes and hugs. It was a joyous occasion, and with the heartbreak, the family had endured over the past year, this was a welcomed surprise.

"Have you two set a date yet?" Marie asked.

"No, everything just happened so fast, we have not discussed any details." Abigail replied.

"I love weddings," Sarah expressed.

"Well, I am glad that you feel that way because I am going to need all the help I can get!" Abigail exclaimed.

"I am a pretty good seamstress so that I can make your gown." Cleo declared. Since entering school, Cleo's speech had dramatically improved. She worked extremely hard to make sure that it did.

"And I am a great cook, so I would be happy to do the food," Sarah stated.

"And I will do the flowers and help with the planning." Marie offered.

"And Jacob and I will hep with settin' up eva thang and handle the music," Nathaniel stated.

Overjoyed with the amount of love and assistance they were receiving with their impending nuptials, Peter and Abigail were both brought to tears.

"Thank you all that would be wonderful, I am overwhelmed by your kindness," Abigail declared.

"Well, you are family now, and if there is one thing about this family you should know, it's that we take care of our own," Sarah said with her hands lovingly on Abigail's shoulders.

After everyone had given the happy couple their heartfelt congratulations, they enjoyed a delicious meal and toasted the happy couple. The celebration lasted well into the night, and Abigail along with all the other guests elected to just remain at John and Marie's for the night.

When everyone was all settled in, Marie looked at all her family, sleeping peacefully under one roof. Even though she was happy for Peter and Abigail, it was bittersweet, because John Jr. was not here to celebrate as well. The thought brought tears of sadness to her eyes. She wiped her tears and tried to focus on the happiness of the day. Marie prayed that whatever John Jr was doing at that very moment, he was safe. She hoped that he knew he was loved and that no matter what happened, he could always come back home.

Chapter Twenty-Eight

After the Dark, Comes the Light

Nate and Sarah had decided that they were going to remain in Canada with their family and when Marie felt better, they moved into their own little house right next door to Jacob and Annie who were expecting their first child. Annie had graduated from college and was now a teacher at a school initially started to instruct the children of escaped slaves but was now open to all children. Nate went to work with Jacob at the Lumber Mill, and Sarah went to work with Annie helping with the children. Sarah loved her work and made a decent living doing it.

The family had received letters from John Jr., in the beginning, letting everyone know how he was coming along in New Orleans; but over time they slowed and then stopped altogether. Marie could only pray that nothing had happened to him. He sent specific instructions for his parents to not contact him after several months. He said he didn't want anyone to find their letters and learn about the secret of his race. He also needed to distance himself from his past to fully embrace his future.

Although it broke their heart, John and Marie agreed. They knew that it was still very perilous in America, especially for a Black man that has been passing as White. They did not want to put any undue danger in their son's path.

Marie had begun to come back to be her usual self again, well as close to normal as one could be after everything she had endured. She began to smile again and resolved to place John Jr. in God's hands. Marie thought of him every day and prayed for his safety, but she no longer let the pain consume her. The love and support of her family, along with the help of Abigail, helped her find her way out of the darkness; and every day she stepped further into the light.

Marie was keeping herself busy helping plan the wedding. It was a happy distraction. The twins' birthday was coming up again, so Marie was working extra hard to make sure she did not let the memory of what happened last year pull her back into the darkness. TJ thought that a big party would only be a painful reminder that John Jr. was no longer there, so he decided he did not want a huge celebration, just a simple dinner with his family.

Marie was up early the morning of TJ's birthday celebration; she decided she was not going to allow the pain of one of her sons not being there, to prevent her from fully celebrating the other. She asked all the family to gather that morning for a day of festivities. Marie was in the kitchen preparing a huge breakfast to kick off her son's special day. The aroma of bacon, eggs, ham, potatoes, and pancakes filled the air and brought everyone to the kitchen.

"It smells delicious in here sweetheart," John said kissing Marie on the cheek.

Peter emerged next drawn by the sweet smells. "Marie darling, I can think of no better way to awake from a night's sleep than by smell of your cooking, Peter stated.

"Thank you, Daddy Pete, now if I could just get the birthday boy out of bed," Marie replied.

"Oh, he will be up soon enough, no one can sleep for long with the smell of all that good food floating through the air," Peter said.

During their conversation, there was a knock at the door, and John went to answer it. Nathaniel, Sarah, Abigail, Jacob, Annie, and Cleo had arrived for the birthday breakfast.

"Good morning everyone," Marie said placing the food on the table.

"Good morning to you my darling girl, everything looks and smells delicious," Sarah said, removing her coat and hat.

"Thank you, my cooking apparently is not enough to raise my son out of bed, so if someone could just go and wake the birthday boy we can get started," Marie quipped.

"I'll go fetch him, Ms. Marie," Cleo volunteered.

"Thank you, sweetheart," Marie replied.

Cleo opened the door to see TJ still sleeping soundly. She stopped for a minute and just watched him sleeping so peacefully. Cleo never imagined that her trip with Helena to reclaim her life would give Cleo a whole new one.

"Happy birthday sleepyhead," Cleo said kissing TJ to wake him.

"Now that is how I want to wake up every morning," TJ said gabbing Cleo for another kiss.

Cleo giggled and happily obliged him. After lovingly holding each other for a moment, Cleo revealed her mission for being there in the first place.

"Your mother sent me to get you up for breakfast," Cleo reported.

"She summoned you all the way over here to wake me up," TJ joked.

"No, silly. We are here to celebrate your birthday," Cleo replied.

"We? Who else is here?" TJ quizzed.

"Everybody, now come on," Cleo said with a huge smile and pulled TJ to his feet.

Moments later, TJ emerged from his room with Cleo to see his entire family sitting at the table.

"Happy Birthday TJ!" They all shouted as an astonished TJ looked around at the people he loved the most in the world.

"What are you all doing here? What is all of this? I thought we were just going to have a simple dinner since John Jr. was not here," TJ quizzed.

"Son you are just as important and loved as John Jr., and just because he chose not to be here with us, does not mean that we are not going to celebrate you," Marie declared.

"I don't know what to say. Thank you all for loving me. I can think of no greater gift to have, than the love of a family," TJ replied.

"Oh son, we love you too. Now come on over here and sit down so we can get to this delicious food!" Peter quipped.

Everyone laughed and took their seats. They filled their bellies with food and their hearts with love and laughter. After breakfast, the family bundled up and went to the town square. There was a festival that day in town. The streets exploded with music, vendors, and performers. The sounds of children of all races, laughing and playing together filled the air and reminded TJ why his parents risked everything to bring them to Canada in the first place. Marie and John wanted their children to know what it was like to have a childhood. This line of thinking caused TJ to think about his brother, and he began to get sad.

"Hey, you OK?" Cleo asked when she saw the sudden change in TJ's demeanor.

Almost like she had a crystal ball into his thoughts, she squeezed his hand and said, "Today is your birthday too, and we will have none of this sadness. Your brother made his choice, and even though he chose not to live here anymore, you cannot choose to stop living your life."

TJ bent down and softly kissed Cleo. He knew that she was right. TJ loved his brother, but he could not follow in his mother's footsteps and let John Jr.'s decision pull him into a place of sadness. He resolved to shake off those feelings of sadness and embrace the joyfulness of the day.

The family moved through the rest of the day, enjoying each other and the festival. When evening began to creep in, it was time to return to Marie and John's house to enjoy TJ's birthday dinner and cake. Everyone entered the house and put their coats away, while John made a fire in the fireplace. Sarah and Cleo helped Marie put the dinner on the table and bring out the cake.

"So how are you enjoying your birthday so far son," Peter asked.

"It's been a wonderful day grandpa. I was amazed. I expected a simple dinner, not an entire day with the people that I love. I am truly blessed," TJ replied.

"Well, we are all blessed son. You are more of a blessing than any of us could have asked for, and I am proud to call you my grandson," Peter declared through tears that were beginning to form.

"Now, we will have no tears today, only laughter and love," Sarah said grabbing Peter by the hand.

"You are right Sarah; lets get to the second delicious meal of today. It may be TJ's birthday, but that is a present we can all enjoy!" Peter quipped trying to get back into a jovial spirit.

Once Marie set the table, the family all took their seats for dinner. They talked about the sights and sounds they experienced that day at the festival. In the end, Marie brought out the cake, and everyone sang Happy Birthday. TJ blew out his candles and cut the first slice.

While everyone was sampling TJ's cake, John started bringing out the birthday gifts. The first one was a leather wallet from Jacob and Annie.

"Thank you, I don't think I have ever had a genuine leather wallet before," TJ expressed.

"You are most welcome nephew. We wanted you to have something nice to put all that money in you are going to be making when you finish school," Jacob replied.

Next was a hand-carved bookshelf from Nathaniel and Sarah.

"Thank you, grandma, and grandpa; it is beautiful. Making this bookcase must have taken you forever grandpa," TJ marveled.

"You most welcome son, we wanted you ta have a nice place fa all dem law books," Nathaniel stated.

Marie and John presented their son with an engraved leather briefcase, followed by Peter and Abigail's gift of a tailored suit. The gifts TJ's family gave him that night warmed his heart, but it was the last one that he received from Cleo that touched his heart. He was so proud of how she had come to Canada and within a year's time had managed to enroll in school and secure employment.

Cleo had saved up to buy TJ a gorgeous pocket watch that she had seen in the jeweler's window one day in town. She had taken over Annie's old position at the Dumas' house while she finished school so that she could earn a living. She and TJ were also engaged to be married, but they decided they were going to wait until they had both finished school and their house. Jacob and Nathaniel were helping TJ to build a modest home of his own on a plot of land close to his uncle and grandparents.

TJ became emotional when Cleo gave him the watch, his eyes filled with tears. He knew what it took for her to be able to purchase something that expensive for him, and the fact that she loved him that much meant more than any gift he had ever received. After all, the presents were opened, and everyone had their fill of food and cake, they all headed home. Although none of them said the words, they wished a silent Happy Birthday to John Jr. and prayed that whatever he did to celebrate that day, he knew that he was in their thoughts and their hearts.

Chapter Twenty-Nine

Money Can't Buy Love

While TJ and the rest of the Devereux family were celebrating TJ's birthday with modest gifts and a small family dinner, the Marchand's celebrated John Jr.'s birthday in a vastly different manner. Olivia had begun planning what she was going to do for John Jr's birthday the day she learned he was coming to live with them. There was no way she was going to miss an opportunity to throw a lavish party. Planning extravagant parties was something on which Olivia could have built a career if she had any desire to work.

Olivia had called upon the best decorators in the business to transform their home into a place of enchantment and wonder. As her daughter Helena had done so many years ago, Olivia decided to have John Jr.'s birthday party on Halloween. In true New Orleans fashion, the celebration was a masquerade ball with vibrant colors splashed across the ballroom and exquisite foods and drinks from the best vendors in the area. The gold embossed invitations were only for New Orleans' crème del a crème.

Olivia and Alexander spared no expense on their grandson's party, and Olivia micromanaged every detail. The entire month before John Jr's birthday, the Marchand estate was buzzing with vendors coming in and out and Olivia overseeing every aspect. The décor took a month by itself to be created and erected in the ballroom. Helena watched vendors come and go and her parents running around catering to every whim John Jr. expressed. The site was beginning to raise familiar feelings she long held for his parents, hatred, and envy.

Olivia was in the ballroom supervising the vendors. She didn't even notice Helena standing there watching.

"Put that gold statue right over there in the center and drape those silk streamers from post to post. I want everything to be perfect. John Jr's celebration is the most important event that we have ever hosted at the Marchand plantation," Olivia instructed.

"Really mother? The most important event? I don't recall you going to this length for my party when I came home from North Carolina, and you didn't do anything when I came home from the looney bin!" Helena exclaimed.

Tiring of Helena's whining, Olivia sighed and rolled her eyes before turning to face her daughter.

"Helena darling, would you please stop referring to the asylum as the looney bin? It sounds so crass and dreadful," Olivia suggested.

In a sarcastic tone, Helena responded, "I'm sorry if my description doesn't depict sunshine and rainbows, but you know those words just don't come to mind when I remember the humiliation and torture I endured inside those walls."

"Helena dear, I do not have time to do this with you right now. John Jr.'s party is tomorrow night, and I still have so much to do to make sure that everything goes exactly according to plan. Now can you please start acting like a mother and stop acting like a jealous sibling." Olivia stated and walked away to continue preparing for the party.

Helena stood there feeling dejected and ignored. She could not believe that her parent's treated her with no more regard than the servants. She thought about how much she hated Marie and John and how John put a common slave above her. Now their son, a living breathing reminder of John's infidelity, was in her home also being held in higher regard as well.

Helena did not think through the plan to bring John Jr. to New Orleans. Her jealousy so blinded her, she never thought about how she felt about him. Nor did she think about what would happen after she brought him back to America. Since Helena discovered John and Marie had fled to Canada with the boys, she focused on destroying their family and their happiness. She never thought about what impact it would have on her own.

By pretending that John Jr. was her child, Helena had placed herself in a no-win situation. As much as she hated having John and Marie's half-breed love child treated like a prince, she couldn't expose him. To reveal that he was not her son, but the son of her husband and his slave mistress, would make her look like a fool. She would be the laughing stock of New Orleans high society and open a lot of questions she did not want to answer. So, Helena had to accept that she must now lay in the proverbial bed of lies she had made for herself. The thought alone made her run straight for the bottle of whiskey in the parlor. Her problems had become more than wine alone could solve.

Meanwhile, John Jr. was busy adjusting to the new life of a business mogul. Over the past year, his closet had added dozens more custom fit suits and expensive shoes. His social circle was heirs and heiresses. Everything that he wanted, he was provided. The servants were at his beck and call, and more money was at his disposal than he could use but not lose.

With no one to guide his moral compass John Jr. began hanging out and partying with his new rich friends almost every night. He was also squandering his fortune on women and gambling. The night before his birthday was no different. He had been out all night with his friends, and the morning of his birthday he was sleeping off yet another binder. Helena went to his room to wake him.

"Well, good morning. I see we started celebrating our birthday a bit early," Helena said.

Annoyed that she was in his room, John Jr. said, "WE have not been doing anything. I would rather celebrate with a vagabond than celebrate anything with you. Now can you please leave me alone, so I can go back to sleep in peace, thank you," he responded without opening his eyes.

"Well from what I hear the company you keep is only a step up from a vagabond," Helena replied.

"Then they are still ten steps up from you," he replied.

"Don't forget who brought you here. You will show me respect!" Helena demanded.

Sitting up in his bed so he could look Helena in the eyes, John Jr. began to laugh.

"Why should I respect someone who doesn't respect herself? You spent years obsessing over a man who not only did not love you but despised you. Instead of respecting yourself enough to move on and save yourself for someone who might give a damn about you, you slept with the first person who showed you any attention and became sterile because of it," he said nonchalantly.

"To further degrade yourself you accepted and passed off the offspring of your husband and the woman he loved as your own. Even when the man divorced you while you were in the nut house, left the country and married the woman that he loved, you were still obsessed. You traveled to Canada and planned some elaborate scheme to reveal my family's secret at my birthday party and steal me away from my parents to hurt them," he continued.

"Now you stand here in my room one year later trying to ruin yet another birthday. You are miserable, and you are low class. With all your money and breeding you will never be a tenth of the woman my real mother is, and you know it, that is why you hate her so much. You are a perfect example that money cannot buy class, and it cannot buy my love or respect. Now for the last time, get the hell out of my room or better yet, do the world a favor and slit your wrists. That is the best birthday present you could give me," John Jr. suggested.

Looking like her heart, had suddenly shattered into a million pieces Helena said, "You truly are your father's son."

"Excuse me?" he asked.

"There was a time that I tried to please your father, and I asked what I could do to make him happy. He said if I took his razor into my bath that evening and slit my wrists that would make him happy," Helena said somberly.

Showing no compassion, John Jr. responded,

"Well, either my father had a dull razor, or you couldn't even manage to do that right, considering you are still here trying to make everyone as miserable as you are."

Without another word, Helena closed the door and went downstairs to find her father. Alexander was in his study reading some documents.

"Father, I need to speak with you about John Jr.," Helena said bursting into her father's office.

"What is it now Helena," Alexander asked without looking up.

"He is out of control. He is hanging around with scoundrels, drinking, and partying all night and gambling away our hard-earned fortune!" Helena complained.

"There is no need to shout dear, my hearing is perfectly fine, and so is John Jr. The boy is young. He is just getting to know us and getting adjusted to this lifestyle. He is sowing his wild oats as all young men of his stature do. Give him some space to become a man, and the fortune is MY hard-earned money darling. You have never worked for or wanted for anything, so why don't you let me worry about how my money is spent? Get some rest before the party sweetheart, you look tired," Alexander stated going returning to his reading.

Realizing her concerns were falling on deaf ears, Helena went to her room. She drank a glass of whiskey, then laid across her bed and cried until she went to sleep. No one came to check on her until it was time for the party that evening.

John Jr. had begun having the servants bring his meals to his room, so no one even saw him until it was time for his party. He freshened up and dressed in a tailor-made suit straight from Paris, an early birthday gift from his grandparents. He also donned a custom-made mask and imported shoes. He was the picture of a young aristocrat, and he was ready to play the part.

When John Jr. descended the staircase that evening, the ballroom was in full swing. Music was playing, and guests were beginning to arrive. There was a long table designated for gifts that was already filling up quickly. The décor was astounding, Olivia was known to have impeccable taste. Everything was plush and rich in color and even the hors-d'oeuvres were exquisite.

"Mary, you look ravishing tonight. I hope you will save me a dance later," John Jr. stated kissing the hand of a young brunette woman with a curvaceous figure.

"Well, of course, I will," the young woman responded with a slight giggle.

John Jr. continued to mingle with his guests and smile as if he were on top of the world. He had everything anyone could ever want, yet his mind kept wandering to his family. Today was the first birthday that John Jr. and TJ ever spent apart. He started remembering all the birthdays he had in the past with his whole family being together, and although none of his birthdays had been as lavish as this one, he still wasn't pleased.

As the party went on, John Jr. grabbed drink after drink and danced with countless women to dull the pain. Nothing seemed to work, so he just kept drinking and dancing. By the time everyone sang happy birthday, and it was time for him to cut his cake, he was so intoxicated that he passed out.

Alexander had two servants take him up to his room and thanked everyone for coming. He attempted to laugh off his grandson's behavior as overindulging on his birthday, but inside Alexander was realizing what Helena had tried to tell him all along. John Jr. was indeed out of control, and Alexander just hoped he had not ignored his grandson's problem so long, that he was beyond saving.

Wedding Day

Spring 1876

The day of Peter and Abigail's wedding had finally arrived. The Spring flowers were blooming, and everything looked fresh and new. It was the perfect time for a wedding. Marie and the rest of the family had worked hard over the last six months to pull together a wedding to remember.

Abigail had always wanted to get married outside, so the couple got permission to get married in the park where Peter proposed. Nathaniel and Jacob had built a beautiful wedding arch, and Marie had woven beautiful flowers through its trellises. Sarah had prepared a feast fit for a royal wedding and purchased a wedding cake from the area's best baker. Cleo had made a wedding dress that would make a queen jealous, and John had booked the minister. TJ was able to get the orchestra that played at the festival on his birthday and instructed them on the couple's favorite songs.

Everything was in place, down to the very last detail. The only thing left was getting married. The night before the wedding, Abigail stayed at Jacob and Annie's house, so Annie and Cleo could help her get ready the next morning. She was so anxious that she couldn't sleep.

The next morning, she woke as a bundle of nerves and Sarah was summoned to help calm her down.

"I hear we have a pretty nervous bride in here," Sarah said entering the room.

Abigail sat in her robe with her hair in pins curled atop her head.

"Oh, Sarah, Peter is everything I had hoped for but never thought I would find. Neither of us is young anymore, I just don't want to disappoint him," she confessed.

"Disappoint him? How on earth do think you are going to do that," Sarah quizzed.

"I have been an independent woman on my own for a very long time, what if I do not know how to be a good wife," Abigail asked.

"Oh Cher, Peter fell in love with you for your strength and independence. He has had plenty of shallow socialites try to catch his attention, but they could never hold his interest, let alone his heart. But you, Cher, you held both. You are the wife that he wants and that alone makes you a good wife. Now dry those tears and shake off that doubt. We have to get you ready to marry the man God sent, just for you," Sarah said.

Abigail hugged Sarah and said, "Thank you so much, Sarah, you have helped me push away those doubts, and now I am ready to become Mrs. Peter Devereux!"

"Alright, let's get you into your dress," Cleo stated carrying the beautiful, beaded gown and veil.

"Cleo, the dress is so beautiful," Abigail exclaimed.

"A beautiful dress for a beautiful bride," Cleo replied.

The women helped Abiail into her dress and Annie helped her with her hair and makeup. Abigail stared at herself in the mirror; she never remembered looking so beautiful or feeling so loved.

On the other side of town, Peter was getting dressed at John and Marie's house.

"I have tied a million bowties in my day, why am I having so many problems with this one?" Peter said becoming frustrated.

"Because it has been a long time since you had to tie one for your wedding. Here grandpa, let me help you," TJ said.

"Thank you, son. I can't believe I am this nervous," Peter responded.

"Relax dad; you are making the right decision. Women like Abigail do not come along that often, and you have been lucky enough to have it come along twice in your lifetime. That is not something that you take for granted. Mama would want you to be happy. I know right now she is up in heaven smiling down on you, because she knows there is finally someone for you to spend your life with," John said.

"Thank you, son," Peter stated hugging John.

"You're welcome, now let's go get you married," John responded.

The men dressed, then went over to the park to make sure everything was ready for the wedding. The minister was already there, and Peter went to take his place beside him. Shortly afterward, Peter saw Abigail headed toward him. John met her at the beginning of the aisle to escort her. She didn't have any family, so marrying into such a close one was like a dream come true for her.

The guests took their seats, and the orchestra began to play. John led Abigail down the aisle to Peter. Peter was in awe of just how beautiful his bride looked coming towards him. He felt butterflies in his stomach, and his heart was overjoyed. When they reached the end of the aisle, John placed Abigail's hand in Peter's.

The minister asked. "Who giveth this woman to marry this man."

John responded, "I do," and kissed her on the cheek and took his seat.

The minister continued with the ceremony, and everyone was shedding tears of joy. When the minister finally pronounced them man and wife, everyone applauded. The wedding was a joyous occasion and just what the family needed to bring some light back into their lives.

Peter and Abigail ate, drank, and danced the day away. They cut their beautiful cake and remained on cloud nine.

"I love you, Mr. Devereux," Abiail said while dancing with her new husband.

"And I love you, Mrs. Devereux," Peter replied, kissing his new bride.

That evening, the couple spent the night at one of the Inns in town. They enjoyed their complimentary bottle of champagne and basket of fresh fruit and laid in bed sat wrapped in each other's arms. They were so caught up in marital bliss that they didn't think about what was going to happen after they were married.

When Peter came to Canada, he never intended to stay for good. He wanted to warn his family about Helena and see how they were doing, but then he met Abigail and things became more complicated.

Peter had enjoyed his time with his family, and he didn't want it to end, but he knew that he had to return to Tobacco Road and check on his business and home. He also wanted to keep an eye on how John Jr. was doing, so he could keep everyone updated.

It was already difficult for him to leave because most everyone Peter loved in his family was in Canada; but now, someone else in his life was special to him. Peter was not sure that he would be able to be away from his new wife for an extended period, and he had no idea how she felt about leaving her home and practice behind to go with him to America.

Peter knew that it was something that he was going to have to discuss with his new bride and time was of the essence. He had been away longer than expected, and although he had stayed connected through letters, he needed to return to North Carolina to settle his affairs.

Peter had left specific instructions on running his business affairs with his attorney, and he put one of the sharecroppers that he trusted most, in charge of running the farm in his absence. In a perfect world, this would not be a problem, but Peter knew if the wrong people knew that he had left his farm in the hands of a Black man that would be all the invitation needed for trouble to make its way to his doorstep. Peter decided to tackle that discussion tomorrow, that night; he just wanted to bask in happiness and leave the rest of the world outside for now. He knew that the morning would come soon enough, and with it, the harsh reality that in America, love does not conquer hate.

What You Won't Do for Love

The next morning, Abigail and Peter awoke to their first new day as husband and wife. Abigail was smiling and in a complete state of peace. In her mind, nothing could spoil her mood, and Peter certainly didn't want to be the one to change that, but he could not put off the inevitable any longer.

Peter knew that asking Abigail to accompany him to North Carolina was not as simple as taking time away from work. Although Abigail was proud to claim her Black heritage, openly loving a Black woman in America could get you killed, so could passing for White. So, Peter faced a difficult decision. He had grown to love Abigail deeply, and she was now his wife. The thought of being without her was more than he could bear.

"Good morning, Mrs. Devereux," Peter said, softly kissing Abigail.

"I don't think I will ever get tired of hearing that," Abigail moaned as she awoke in her husband's arms.

"Good, because I will never tire of saying it," Peter responded.

Abigail climbed out of bed and looked out the window at the dawn of a new morning.

"Darling, there is something that we need to talk about," Peter stated.

Instantly, Abigail felt a sinking feeling in the pit of her stomach; she knew that they had jumped into marriage and had not fully discussed what their life would be like afterward. Now, she had the feeling the day had come Peter wanted to discuss one of those unsaid details.

"I think I know what it is. You have to go back, don't you?" Abigail asked.

"Yes, I do. I left in such a hurry that I left things unsettled in North Carolina. I have my business and my house there, and I made no provisions to leave North Carolina permanently, but I got here and met you, and suddenly nothing else mattered. You are my wife now, I love you more than my own life, and it would kill me if something happened to you. I do not want to spend one day without you, but America is not like Canada. There are some very evil people there who hate Black people. They also hate White people who fall in love with a Black person, and Black people who they find out are passing for White. Given the danger, I feel it would be selfish to ask you to go with me, but my heart won't let me tell you to stay here," Peter confessed.

Peter told Abigail it would only be temporary and that they would return to Canada once he had successfully settled his business affairs.

Surprisingly, with not one second of hesitation, Abigail responded, "You are my husband. I am yours until death we do part. Where you go, I will follow, even to the depths of hell."

Abigail loved Peter with every fiber of her being, so even though she knew the risks, she agreed to hide her racial identity long enough for Peter to conclude his business in North Carolina. Now, they just had to inform the rest of the family.

Peter and Abigail continued to enjoy the rest of their morning as husband and wife, then headed over to John and Marie's to tell them of their plan to return to North Carolina.

John and Marie had done as Peter requested and summoned the whole family to hear the news Peter expressed was of dire importance. Since Annie was due any day, she usually tried to stay close to home, but she came with everyone else to hear what Peter had to say.

When everyone arrived, the looks on Peter and Abigail's faces told them, this was not going to be a pleasant conversation.

"What's going on Peter?" Sarah asked as she took a seat.

"We have some news that we have to share with everyone, and it may be difficult to hear," Peter declared.

"What is it, dad? You are scaring us now," John stated.

"Well, there is no easy way to say this so, I am going to just have to say it. Abby and I are going back to North Carolina," Peter said.

Everything was silent for a moment, and an eerie feeling crept over the room. Everyone knew that Abigail was Black, and everyone knew what that meant in America, especially in the South. That was the entire reason they all moved to Canada in the first place.

"Dad, don't do this. You know what it is like in America right now, and you are going to go back and take your new Black wife. You would be putting her life in danger; how could you do that? You know we are terrified every day that someone will find out John Jr.'s secret and try to kill him, now you want to add you and Abigail to the list of people we have to worry about?" John questioned.

"John is right, Peter, you just sent your son and his family to Canada to avoid the danger that you are dragging your new wife into!" Sarah shouted.

"He is not dragging me anywhere. I know that you all are concerned for me, but I know the dangers," Abigail stated.

"No, no you don't. You were born here; you have no idea what it is like to live every day in fear that at any moment, for any reason, a White person can just end your life, with no repercussions. You don't know what it is like to be degraded and disrespected simply because of the color of your skin, to have a White man rape you and beat you because he feels that your body is his property! You have no idea the danger you are walking into!" Sarah shouted.

"Hummingbird, let it go. She his wife now, nothing you say gonna keep her from goin' wit him," Nathaniel said.

With all the commotion and tension in the room, the newest member of the family decided to make their entrance. Suddenly Annie let out a loud scream, and a gush of water fell from under her dress.

"My water just broke, the baby is coming!" Annie screamed.

"OK, Jacob, go and put Annie on the bed. I need someone to boil some water and bring me some fresh towels and a sterilized knife to cut the cord," Abigail ordered.

Everyone did as they were instructed and brought Abigail everything she needed.

"Oh my God, this pain is killing me!" Annie screamed.

"You are going to be fine Annie, I am going to look and see how far along you are," Abigail stated.

When Abigail felt between Annie's legs, she noticed that the baby was breeched.

"Ok Annie, whatever you do, do not push. The baby is breeched," Abigail warned.

"Please save my baby, don't let my baby die!" Annie pleaded.

"No one is going to die today, you hear me. Now I need you to listen to me. Stay calm and keep breathing. I am going to try to turn the baby around," Abigail said.

Annie nodded her head and continued to breathe. Jacob held her hand and wiped her head with a cold cloth. Everyone else in the room began to pray.

Abigail worked feverishly to get the baby in the right position, and after what seemed like an eternity, she was able to get the baby in the correct direction.

"OK Annie, now I need you to push as hard as you can. Are you ready?" Abigail asked.

Annie nodded her head while still breathing.

"Alright now push!" Abigail ordered.

Annie pushed as hard as she could, each time on Abigail's command, and after intense and terrifying labor, the new parents welcomed Jacob Nathaniel Monet into the world. Jacob chose the middle name in honor of his father.

"Congratulations! You have a beautiful baby boy!" Abigail stated, wrapping the baby in a blanket and handing him to Annie.

With tears in his eyes, Jacob said "Hey little guy, are we happy to see you. You gave us quite a scare."

Annie couldn't speak, she just held her baby close and kissed him gently on the forehead.

"Thank you for saving my grandson," Sarah stated hugging Abigail.

"Hey, we are family remember, and family sticks together," Abigail said with a smile.

Everyone congratulated the new parents then left them alone to spend some time bonding with their son. They didn't go far, though. Everyone just went into the living room. They wanted to be there to help with the baby and let Annie get some rest.

"I am sorry if I seemed harsh before, I am just concerned for your safety," Sarah offered.

Abigail smiled and replied, "I know, and I appreciate that. I am going to be fine. Peter is going to settle his affairs, check on John Jr. and then we will be back in Canada before you know it."

"My prayers are with you both," Sarah said giving Abigail one last hug.

Returning her embrace, Abigail replied, "Thank you."

For the next couple of weeks, Abigail and Peter spent every day with the family helping with the new baby. Then Peter and Abigail packed up their belongings and prepared to head to North Carolina, but they promised they would return soon.

Although he tried to hide it, the thought of going back to Tobacco Road terrified Peter. He was leaving Canada with the woman that he loved and returning to America, the only home he had ever known. Peter had no idea what was waiting for him upon his return. He had become so engrossed in his happiness in Canada, that his life in America became a distant memory. Now he had to get home to make sure he kept the danger at bay; Peter just hoped that he was not walking right into it and bringing the woman he loved with him.

About the Author

Danielle Siler is a phenomenal author whose fan-favorite book *Secrets on Tobacco Road* first introduced readers to the Devereux, Marchand, and Jean Baptiste (Monet) families. Now, her highly anticipated sequel *My Secret to Keep* is the second installment in her *Secret Chronicles Series*, but it is Siler's fourth book. She currently resides in Washington, DC with her husband and two little girls and works for the government.

Siler is finishing up the sequel to her urban fiction novel, *A Beautiful Lie,* entitled A *Beautiful Death*. Also, she is working on a new series called the *Yancy Childs Diaries*. The debut novel from this series, entitled *God Bless the Child*, is a psychological thriller that follows the cases and life of forensic psychologist, Dr. Yancy Childs. Siler's talent for covering any genre and developing robust characters will leave you on the edge of your seat. Check out all the books in her current series and see why fans are hungry for the next journey.

- ❖ Dreams in Motion: A Collection of Poems and Short Stories

- ❖ Secrets on Tobacco Road

- ❖ A Beautiful Lie

- ❖ My Secret to Keep

- ❖ A Beautiful Death

- ❖ A Beautiful Ending

- ❖ No More Secrets